THE HOLY SINNER:

A Gothic Tale of the Baal Shem Tov

by

BARAK A. BASSMAN

TELEMACHUS PRESS

This book is a work of fiction. Names, characters, places and incidents are either the product of the author's imagination or are used fictitiously. Any resemblance to actual persons, living or dead, or to actual events or locales is entirely coincidental.

THE HOLY SINNER: A GOTHIC TALE OF THE BAAL SHEM TOV
Copyright © 2021 Barak A. Bassman. All rights reserved, including the right to reproduce this book, or portions thereof, in any form. No part of this text may be reproduced, transmitted, downloaded, decompiled, reverse engineered, or stored in or introduced into any information storage and retrieval system, in any form or by any means, whether electronic or mechanical without the express written permission of the author. The scanning, uploading, and distribution of this book via the Internet or via any other means without the permission of the author and publisher is illegal and punishable by law. Please purchase only authorized electronic editions and do not participate in or encourage electronic piracy of copyrighted materials.

The publisher does not have any control over and does not assume any responsibility for author or third-party websites or their content.

Cover designed by Telemachus Press, LLC

Cover art:
Copyright © iStockPhoto521579031/stanciuc

Publishing Services by Telemachus Press, LLC
7652 Sawmill Road
Suite 304
Dublin, Ohio 43016
http://www.telemachuspress.com

ISBN: 978-1-956867-05-3 (eBook)
ISBN: 978-1-956867-06-0 (Paperback)

Library of Congress Control Number: 2021921432

Version 2021.10.19

Table of Contents

THE HOLY SINNER:

A Gothic Tale of the Baal Shem Tov

I. A Most Unlikely Match

ZALMAN THE BLACKSMITH was not accustomed to receiving good news, as his life in the *shtetl* of W. usually consisted of abuse from the master smith whom he served, abuse from the storekeepers whom he could barely pay, and abuse from anyone else who happened to notice him shuffle by with his downcast eyes. He was young—barely fifteen—but already had the stooped back and despairing sighs of an old man long defeated by life's disappointments.

But on this day, the master smith told him something extraordinary: Zalman was no longer to be an apprentice smith eking out a meager living. In fact, he was no longer to be an artisan at all. For who knows what crazy reason, his master continued, Raizel, the wealthy and beautiful young widow who had rejected so many proposed marriage matches with the finest families in Poland, had that very morning informed both the master smith and the rabbi that she wished to wed none other than the ignoramus *schlemiel* blacksmith Zalman.

Zalman was sure the master smith was mocking him. After his hopes would be raised foolishly, stupidly, they would be quickly dashed amidst peals of roaring laughter. He could easily imagine what was going to happen: Every drunk artisan would greet him with an exaggerated *mazel tov* to the bridegroom, before snickering again at his idiocy for even believing for a minute that a match with a woman such as the widow Raizel could happen to the likes of him.

So he replied harshly to the master smith: It is not funny to joke about matches. I won't fall for your lies and tricks.

But his master swore that he spoke the truth—the widow Raizel wanted Zalman as her groom and no one else. Zalman, in turn, grew angrier and repeated that he would not be taken in by this hoax.

Eventually the master smith stormed out and returned an hour later with the rabbi, who confirmed that the widow Raizel did in fact wish to marry Zalman. Although he briefly considered whether the rabbi could also be trying to trick him, there seemed to be no reason why the rabbi would do so—the rabbi was a kind man and too proud to sully his reputation by joining in the pranks of unlearned artisans.

Zalman now started to believe that this match could really happen. He tried to recall what Raizel looked like. He had seen her before—the *shtetl* of W. being a smallish town, every Jew had seen every other Jew at some time or other—but they were guilty, stolen glances, the way he would take a quick, furtive look at a grand Polish lady, so rich and pretty and lavishly dressed. Raizel wore an elegant wig, of course, and finely made, but modest, black dresses that did not reveal too much of the shape of her figure. Her eyes, though, he recalled those eyes—narrow but dark blue, which seemed to be burning and glowing.

Zalman reviewed the few facts he knew about her life. Raizel's father had been the wealthiest merchant in town, with extensive leaseholds from the Polish nobleman who owned these lands. She had been his only child. Her mother had died in childbirth and, heartbroken, her father had refused to remarry.

Only the best match would do for his lovely daughter, and he had traveled from yeshiva to yeshiva throughout Poland and Lithuania searching for a Talmudic prodigy who would be worthy of her hand. The lure of an immense dowry and a beautiful bride had attracted much interest, but he still rejected match after match—impressive though the boys may have been, they were still not good enough.

Finally, in Vilna, the proud *tate* found the perfect bridegroom for his Raizel, a boy named Gershon. This Gershon was not only the most renowned Talmud prodigy in Lithuania, but he also had great *yiches*, being descended from a long line of distinguished rabbis all the way back, so the family claimed, to the famed Moshe Isserles of blessed memory. And if all that were not enough, he was as handsome as the shining sun.

But then everything had gone wrong. The first sign of trouble was that, even though a year had passed since the wedding, Raizel had yet to become pregnant. And then, just as tongues had started wagging about her barrenness, Gershon fell ill. The illness spread to Raizel's father, too, and both men were dead within a week.

The town was shocked. Why were such righteous, learned men, pillars of their generation, struck down so cruelly? Had they secretly sinned in some way? Or maybe the angels had yearned for their sweet company in the World to Come?

Still, Raizel was so young, and so wealthy, that everyone assumed she would quickly remarry. Matchmakers descended like locusts upon W., offering this rich man's son or that well-known scholar, but she refused them all. Zalman recalled overhearing women stifle a tear as they lamented her sad fate—poor thing, they would say, she is too heartbroken to try again.

But now his fate was suddenly bound up with hers. The day after the master smith's startling message, Zalman was summoned to the rabbi's house to sign the agreement of betrothal. Raizel did not attend, but she had sent a male relation as her representative, a bent old man with hateful eyes.

Although the rabbi read out the betrothal terms slowly and clearly, Zalman still could not make heads or tails of the flowery rabbinical Hebrew and asked for the contract to be translated for him into simple Yiddish. Raizel's relation shook his head and sighed loudly—no doubt, Zalman thought, he could not believe that the beautiful and distinguished Raizel wished to marry such a fool. Nevertheless, the kindly rabbi obliged Zalman and explained the terms in a straightforward Yiddish that any Jew could understand.

And what terms they were: Raizel agreed to pledge all her wealth, including the control of her father's many business enterprises and leaseholds, as her dowry. The only obligation upon Zalman was to renounce his vocation as an impoverished apprentice blacksmith in favor of becoming a wealthy merchant. He laughed aloud at this clause—as if he would spurn such riches so he could continue fixing horseshoes and breathing soot.

After the betrothal agreement was signed, the master smith excused Zalman from his duties at the forge to focus on getting ready for the wedding, which was to be held in only two months' time. But Zalman was not able to enjoy his newfound leisure. He lost track of all his trips to the tailor to be outfitted with a new wardrobe appropriate both for the wedding and for his new station in life. He was shuttled around to meet with the various merchants who drew their livelihoods from serving the interests of Raizel's family. And he met repeatedly with the rabbi, who painstakingly helped him to compose a simple but respectable Talmudic discourse to deliver on the morning of his wedding, on the *aggadot* told about the holy sages of blessed memory and in particular the righteousness of Rabbi Akiva's saintly wife.

When the day of the wedding arrived, and Raizel's veil was uplifted so he could see her face (lest he be fooled like Jacob into marrying Leah instead of Rachel), Zalman was stunned: He had never beheld such a beautiful woman—her blood red lips, her dark blue eyes, filled him with aching, inchoate desires.

The rest of the day was a blur. Zalman nervously delivered his discourse on the righteousness of Rabbi Akiva's wife, word for word as he had memorized it, and then was whisked away before any of the town's more educated men could question him on it. The wedding ceremony itself went by so fast that he could hardly believe it had really happened.

At the reception, he drank toast after toast, to his health and good fortune, to his wife's health and good fortune, and to many other persons' health and good fortunes too, resulting in him becoming quite drunk. When a parade of wealthy and distinguished men approached his seat to congratulate him, Zalman did his best to steady his slurring speech and spew out appropriate words of thanks and gratitude.

He thought how absurd this all was: He, Zalman, a second-rate (at best) apprentice blacksmith, ignorant, poor, had now just become the richest man in town and was being shown honor by the most eminent householders. More than honor: They were currying favor with him—with him!—the *schlemiel* who could barely mend a horseshoe, and whose great ambition had once been to acquire a small smithy of his own somewhere and some willing Jewish bride, no matter how poor or ugly, so long as she could bear children and offer a kind word now and then.

He was certain he would wake up and this silly fantasy would vanish before his eyes. But on it went, toast after toast, gift after gift, and so many requests from so many Jews for help and money discreetly whispered into his ear.

II. How Fortune Had
Come to Favor Zalman

THROUGHOUT THE WEDDING reception, Zalman did not speak to his bride. Between the toasts and the wedding jesters and the crush of well-wishers, he had not had a moment's peace to ask her how she was or, more importantly, why she had chosen to pluck him out of his filthy smithy into such wealth and prominence.

But the celebration eventually ended. Zalman was then escorted by his new servants to his new home, an imposing three-story stone building on the main square across from the church with the high spires. The rooms on the first floor, the servants explained to him, were for conducting business. The second floor contained the master's bedroom, where they left him to await his bride.

In short order, Raizel also entered the room. Although Zalman had known this moment would come, he was still terrified. Unsure exactly what to do, he stood there, fully dressed, gawking at her like she was some magical treasure washed up from the sea.

She smiled and removed her wig and hairpins, letting her natural thick black hair fall wildly about her shoulders and chest.

Next, she slipped out of her wedding gown, which she let fall carelessly onto the floor. Stripped now to her undergarments, Raizel approached her groom and put her arms around his neck.

Zalman was powerfully aroused, but also frozen with fear. He kept telling his limbs to move, but they would not budge. Raizel laughed softly and helped him out of his clothes. She took his hand, led him to the bed, and, after pinning him securely underneath her body, consummated the marriage.

Afterwards, Zalman felt a wave of relaxation wash over him, which finally gave him the courage to speak.

Raizel, he said, why me? You had your pick of grooms with wealth, learning, pedigree, certainly someone more handsome. So why choose me?

Raizel rolled over and rested her head on his chest. I am glad you asked, she said. I could tell this was troubling you. You have been asking yourself this question ever since we were betrothed, I am sure, but I wanted to wait until this moment, on our wedding night, to tell you the answer. It is a marvelous story that shows how the Holy One, Blessed be He, works in mysterious and wondrous ways. For you see, I married you because we were destined from birth to be a match—the Heavenly Court itself had decreed that you and I were to be wed in this life. If only my father, may his memory be a blessing, had respected the will of *HaShem*, he would have been with us today to celebrate.

I have always known that there was only one man destined to be my bridegroom. When I would play with the other little girls, they would prattle on about the kinds of husbands they would marry someday—maybe he would be rich, or a scholar, or handsome, or maybe he would, may it never happen to us, be a violent drunk. But when it was my turn to talk about my future husband, I would just say that the Holy One, Blessed be He, had already picked my match and I was merely waiting for him to appear.

Why was I so sure that my future had been arranged for me? I do not know. It simply felt like the truth, like the way you are sure that the sun will rise and set. And it did not bother me: My future husband was fixed, like a star in the night sky, and that was that. No point in fussing over the matter.

When I became a woman, my father told me he would accept only the finest match as my groom. He swore there was no girl in Poland as beautiful as me or with such a large dowry—no need to settle for anything less than the best of the best.

But I told him what I knew to be true in the depths of my soul: My *bashert*, my destined one, had already been chosen for me. We had only to wait for him to arrive. Haggling over possible matches with other men was a silly waste of everyone's time.

My father could not believe what I was saying. How will we know who your prince is? he asked me. Will he carry a letter of introduction from the Heavenly Court explaining how you two have been destined for each other since birth? Stop this nonsense: Matches are made by the fathers of the bride and the groom, not by childish daydreams.

So he went forth out into the world to find me a match, but something would go wrong each time. This fine scholar turned out to be a drunkard, another was too poor, or this third one lied about his family lineage. No one was good enough.

Finally, in his frustration and despair, he took me with him to Mezhbizh to seek the counsel of Rabbi Israel ben Eliezer, the Baal Shem Tov. Have you heard of the wonders of this holy sage, this *tzaddik*? He has studied the secrets of the *Kabbalah* far more deeply than any other man, and he can perceive the truths obscured beneath the surface illusions all around us. No other *baal shem* can wield the magical holy names and command the powerful spirits of angels and demons as he can. My father assured me that if any sage could solve the riddle of the right match for me, it was the Baal Shem Tov.

After we arrived in Mezhbizh, my father arranged for us to have an audience with him. On the appointed day, right after breakfast, we rode in a wagon to the house at the edge of town where the Baal Shem Tov lives. His wife invited us in, served brandy and honey cakes, and told us to wait in the kitchen until the holy sage was ready to receive us.

We waited for a long time in that kitchen. Every so often we would hear the strangest sounds coming from behind the door of the Baal Shem Tov's study. Sometimes there was howling; sometimes jubilant song; and sometimes he sounded as if he was arguing with several different people, even though we had been told that he was alone. Doubtless seeing how confused our faces were, his wife calmly explained that from time to time her husband's soul ascends to the higher realms to debate with the angels in the Heavenly Court and plead on behalf of the Jews of the world.

Eventually we were ushered into the *tzaddik*'s presence.

Rabbi, my father began, I have come . . .

But the Baal Shem Tov interrupted him and said: I know why you have come. You wish to understand why you cannot find the right match for your daughter. You think to yourself, like any proud *tate*, a beautiful girl, in the flower of her youth, should be wed to a righteous bridegroom and start a family. But you have looked for a bridegroom in all the wrong places, because your eyes can see only illusions—fleeting wealth, the arid learning of so-called scholars, puffed up claims of distinguished family lineage. You have ignored the deeper spiritual truths through which the Holy One, Blessed be He, reveals His light and His guidance.

I prayed this morning to be given the knowledge of what should be done with your Raizel. But something was blocking my vision—I could not clearly see the root of her soul. So I invoked a combination of holy names to summon a high-ranking angel to my study to explain this matter to me. The angel made excuses and evaded my questions, until I uttered far more terrible holy names and bound him in fetters. I swore he would not be released until the truth of Raizel's match was revealed to me.

The angel begged me not to force him to tell what had been decreed for her match, because he was afraid I would be upset with him. No doubt, said the angel, you think such a beautiful and esteemed maiden would be betrothed only to the most handsome and learned young Jew in all of Poland, but that is not the case, and I cannot tell you why.

I said to the angel: I don't care if you tell me why—I shall leave the why to the Holy One, Blessed be He, in His infinite wisdom and mercy. But I must know who. Whoever has been chosen, reveal his name to me, so I can make the match.

But the angel still hesitated to speak the young man's name, and so I uttered yet another curse to tighten his fetters and drive sharp spikes into his soft wings.

And when he could finally bear his suffering no longer, the angel at last spoke the name of the true destined match, the *bashert*, for your Raizel. Your son-in-law shall be none other than: Zalman the Blacksmith. He will move to your town soon, as an apprentice to serve the master smith. When he arrives, you must go to him immediately, before he considers another bride, make the match, and all will be well for you and your daughter.

My father exploded with rage. He said that he had not traveled so far from home to be mocked and ridiculed. He swore that he *would* match me with the most handsome and the most learned Jew he could find, because I deserved nothing less.

The Baal Shem Tov sighed sadly. He said to my father: You think you are wise, because you have great riches and because you raise your voice at anyone who dares to show you the error of your ways. But your wealth and your life can vanish in the blink of an eye if *HaShem* wills it. The decree of the Heavenly Court will be carried out, and Raizel shall wed Zalman the Blacksmith. If you try to marry her to another, the wrath of the Holy One, Blessed be

He, shall be upon you. Any other bridegroom but Zalman shall surely die soon after the wedding, and before any child is conceived. And who knows? Perhaps the Lord of Hosts will not spare you either, arrogant rich fool.

Hearing these words, my father grabbed my wrist, dragged me out of the holy saint's study, and we returned home. He then sent for a matchmaker and arranged my betrothal to a bridegroom who was perfect in every respect—handsome, learned, rich, and with an impeccable lineage. My father promised his new son-in-law that he would never need to work, only study, and that my father would build a magnificent new yeshiva for him to preside over—he spoke proudly of the many eager disciples who would flock to learn at his son-in-law's feet in the years to come.

Still, I was worried. The words of the Baal Shem Tov had penetrated deeply into my soul. I knew he was speaking the truth. I cannot say how I knew this, but I felt my heart nod in vigorous agreement when the holy *tzaddik* spoke your name.

On our wedding night, my bridegroom was not able to perform the duties of a husband. He told me I was beautiful, he quoted verses from the Song of Songs to praise my loveliness, but his flesh ignored these fine words and would not respond as it was supposed to. During our first few nights together I tried everything I could to entice a reaction from his body, but nothing worked.

My husband soon fled from my bed, preferring to spend his days and nights swaying before the Talmud, sleeping on a bench in the study house, and only coming home—briefly—to eat just enough food to keep body and soul stitched together.

He refused to speak to me.

I wept many times in my loneliness. But then my father would upbraid me harshly—why was I crying, I had been blessed with a husband so righteous that he could not break free from his holy studies even for a moment—I should feel proud to be the wife of such a scholar.

But I felt no pride in my marriage. I was angry with myself for not being able to please my husband, and I begged the Holy One, Blessed be He, to restore my husband to my bed and to help him to do what was necessary so I could have a child.

Yet my prayers were wasted. The terrible prophecy of Rabbi Israel ben Eliezer, the holy Baal Shem Tov, came true: Barely a year after we were wed, my husband was struck dead by a sudden illness—and my father too.

I was drowning in my grief and sorrow. The matchmakers again stampeded to my door, swearing this or that perfect bridegroom would bring joy back to my heart.

But I rejected them all.

Then one evening I had the most extraordinary dream. I was walking alone through the town at night. It was quiet. A star fell from the sky and landed right in front of me. It was so bright that, at first, I had to avert my eyes, but when I was able to look upon it, I saw Rabbi Israel ben Eliezer, the Baal Shem Tov, standing before me.

Have you forgotten the words I spoke to you? he said. Your *bashert*, your destined one, is here now, in this town. Zalman the Blacksmith is here. Seek him out, marry him at once, and the will of the Holy One, Blessed be He, shall be done.

Then I woke with a start. The next morning, I summoned the rabbi, and made the match.

III. The First Stumble Downwards

ZALMAN SETTLED INTO his new life as a wealthy and important man. He was given charge of the vast business enterprises that Raizel's father and grandfather had built. He was also, as the town's richest man, appointed to a number of positions of communal authority, including serving as one of the trustees of the Jewish community's charitable funds for the support of beggars, the care of the infirm, and the provision of dowries for orphan girls.

The world seemed to be turned upside down. Where once he had awoken to the master smith boxing his ears for sleeping too much and working too little, now he was gently stirred from his slumbers by nervously smiling servants carrying trays of tea and biscuits and jam. When he walked down the street, everyone stepped aside to let him pass. In the synagogue, he no longer prayed in a back corner, but was seated in a place of honor by the Eastern Wall, where the town's rabbi and prosperous householders greeted him warmly and asked politely after his business and his health.

And his Raizel was a wonder. Before his wedding day, Zalman had never touched a woman; his only sensual pleasure had been stealing glances at pretty women and hoping desperately that no one noticed what he was doing. But now, he whiled away his nights with the most beautiful woman in the town, greedily nibbling at her moist, thick lips and running his hands all over her soft hips and thighs.

Raizel was also invaluable in running the household. She bossed around the servants, made sure the pantry was well stocked, supervised repairs to the house, and picked out new horses for the stable. Zalman thanked the Holy One, Blessed be He, for the blessing of such a superbly competent wife.

Nevertheless, Zalman could not rely on his wife to do everything for him, much as he would have liked to. He was expected to manage the business that had come with his wife's dowry. Raizel's father and grandfather had built their wealth primarily by leasing timber rights from the local Polish count. His Lordship owned vast tracts of forest land and needed a capable agent to cut down the trees, finish the timber into planks, and transport the planks across the roads and rivers of Poland to the larger markets in Europe— particularly as the *Pan* himself was usually not resident on his estates, preferring instead his elegant villa in Warsaw. In exchange for leasing the timber rights on the Count's estates, there was a large, fixed annual payment due to the His Lordship. But so long as the business was run well, the profits were immense.

Unfortunately, Zalman did not understand anything about running a timber business—how to hire good workers, how to choose the right trees to cut down, where to ship the finished wood, or what price to ask. He asked the employees who had served Raizel's father for their guidance, and while, at first, they were helpful, they soon lost patience with their new master and gave increasingly curt answers to his endless questions.

Zalman could feel their contempt for him, a young boy—a foolish *yingele*—in over his head, but he was not sure what else he could do. If he were to turn to Raizel and ask her to run the business for him, how much of a good-for-nothing would he be then?

She was already run ragged managing their large household. And he was not like her first husband, a great scholar who needed relief from the pressures of earning a living so he could spend days and nights poring over holy texts. He was, Zalman reminded himself, a barely literate ignoramus who struggled to read the Psalms and had never studied a page of Talmud in his life.

If he was not working at the timber business, and if he had no studies to turn to instead, then what would he be doing with his time? He could not go back to being a blacksmith—he was a rich man now, not a dirty artisan, and had to behave suitably to his station in life. But he had no clue how to do what was expected of him in his new role.

Still, he had to try. He trudged out to the forests with his work crews and made bold decisions, with an air of breezy confidence, about which trees to chop down, praying silently that he had not just done something completely stupid. And the Ukrainian peasants whom he employed obeyed his dictates without question. Zalman tried to convince himself that this was because these seasoned timber cutters were impressed with his intuitive and keen judgment.

Yet it was a different part of the business that would prove to be his undoing. In order to transport the finished logs to the great cities of Germany and beyond, Raizel's father and grandfather had relied on brokers who would buy the wood from them and then resell it elsewhere. One of these brokers was a boisterous bear of a man named Menachem. This Menachem took Zalman under his wing. He offered pointers about the timber trade and warned Zalman to be careful of people who would try to cheat him— watch the foreman leading the crews in the forest, he would say, make sure he does not skim any of the timber to sell later as firewood. And he would warn Zalman about the other brokers, who always pretended the prices in the big cities were much lower than was really the case in order to beat down their purchase price from Zalman—they will steal your rightful profits, he would say.

Zalman listened in rapture to Menachem's words. He finally had a friend, someone on his side trying to help him. His feelings of terrified incompetence and isolation would fade away when he drank in Menachem's confident advice and felt the older man's sweaty, hairy hand on his shoulder.

When Zalman began to offer his own tentative thoughts on the timber business, Menachem would enthusiastically agree with his observations and express astonishment that such a young man, with so little experience, could have such penetrating insight. Menachem would declare Zalman to be a prodigy in business and insist they drink a toast of vodka in celebration of his tremendous talents. Encouraged by Menachem's words—after all, as a man who had spent his whole life in the timber trade, he should know what he was talking about—Zalman swelled with pride and fancied himself a cunning and sharp merchant, the sort of man who could not be trifled with—no scholar, it was true, but nonetheless an imposing man of commerce.

And then one day, after a few too many joyous toasts had left Zalman lightheaded and tipsy, Menachem confided that he had run into a problem and needed Zalman's wise counsel. Of course, anything for my dear friend, Zalman replied.

Menachem smiled deferentially and thanked him humbly. He then explained that one of the places where he resold his timber was Danzig. In Danzig, he dealt with his cousin Mordkhe. He had always trusted this Mordkhe and judged him to be a good and honest man. But Mordkhe had taken advantage of Menachem's good nature. Mordkhe claimed his customers were late in paying him and so he, in turn, could not yet pay Menachem. He asked Menachem to extend him credit so he could continue to purchase the fine wood that Menachem supplied. Menachem agreed at once. But Mordkhe—may he be cursed, the thieving *mamzer*—never paid up, but rather kept taking more and more timber on credit. Finally, too late, Menachem realized he had been swindled and summoned Mordkhe to court to demand payment. But by then Mordkhe had disappeared without a trace.

So you see, my dear friend Zalman, how I have been undone by my generous and charitable nature. I am ruined now—I have no capital left to buy your timber, and if I cannot buy, then I cannot make a profit by reselling. I have three daughters who will soon be old enough to marry—but how will I give them dowries now? Who will want a bankrupt fool as a father-in-law? What should I do, Zalman? Advise me, please.

Zalman immediately offered to sell Menachem as much timber as he needed on credit—take it, he said, use it to get back on your feet, and when you are ready to pay me back, then you can pay me back. I will not turn my back on a dear friend.

Menachem, with tears streaming down his cheeks, thanked Zalman profusely and called down many blessings upon his head. Zalman had never felt so proud of himself.

But then many weeks went by without Menachem paying for the timber he had taken on credit. Zalman would gently ask Menachem when he would be paid, but there was always an excuse at hand—his customers were going to pay him next week, his horse had died and he had needed to buy a new one, or his agent had been sent with the money and would surely arrive any day now.

Zalman let himself be soothed by these excuses. Everything would be fine, he told himself. Menachem is a good man, a righteous man, and I should not be a greedy miser squeezing him for every last ducat. He has given sound reasons for why he cannot pay now—reasons that men of business like us well understand—but soon enough he will pay what he owes, and all will be well.

Yet the days dragged on without payment. Finally, Zalman's bookkeeper confronted him and insisted that Menachem be cut off.

The bookkeeper showed Zalman the staggering extent of his losses from having given away so much timber on credit without having ever received any payment in return.

Zalman felt his knees buckle and his heart sink. He quickly scrawled out a note to Menachem, explaining that he needed to see him immediately and could no longer wait for payment. But after the note was delivered, Menachem failed to appear. When Zalman tried to find him the next day, there was no trace of Menachem, and no one knew where he had gone.

And then Zalman received even more bad news: a brusque letter from His Lordship the Count demanding payment of the fee for the lease of the timber rights upon his estates. But with his losses from Menachem's theft, Zalman could not pay the huge sum owed. He was ruined—the Count would strip him of the leasehold, seize his assets, maybe even imprison him. He would surely be beaten by the Count's servants, to show everyone what happened to Jews who failed to pay their *Pan* what was owed.

Zalman now cursed the day he had been betrothed to Raizel. This is what comes, he told himself, from aspiring to honors you do not merit. Wealthy learned men know how to run a business, not stupid ignorant artisans. He should have stayed where he belonged in the smithy and married an artisan's daughter. But instead, fool that he was, he had jumped at the opportunity to seize riches beyond his station and thus had come to a well-deserved state of ruin.

Zalman steeled himself to confess his failings to Raizel. That night, after dinner, he asked to speak with her privately, away from the servants. Haltingly and tearfully, he explained what had happened, how he had been duped, and how they were now ruined. He told Raizel he would write to His Lordship the Count the next morning to explain everything that had happened and that he could not satisfy the payment owed on the leasehold for the timber rights. He would take complete responsibility for his foolishness and beg for mercy on her behalf.

When he was finished, Raizel bent over his quivering body curled up in the chair, held his hands, and let her thick hair brush against Zalman's cheeks and throat. She spoke to him softly, in a voice full of love:

My dear, sweet husband, we are not ruined. Our debt to the *Pan* for the leasehold will be paid. Have you forgotten that we were matched by the Heavenly Court itself? Do you think the Holy One, Blessed be He, brought about our marriage only so our lives would collapse into misery and poverty?

Until three months ago, you could easily pay the debt owed on the leasehold. At that time, if you remember, you made a generous donation to the community funds for the support of the poor, the infirm, and the dowries of orphan girls. If you had that money back again, you would have no worries.

Now you are thinking that money is gone, already donated and accounted for, so how could you have it back again? But you are forgetting that you are also a trustee of the community funds. You can simply borrow back the funds you donated, pay the *Pan*, and then repay the community once our profits return to what they have always been. No one will notice the difference.

Zalman looked up at his Raizel in shock. How can you suggest such a thing, to steal from the poor? To take food from their mouths?

But Raizel merely sighed and stroked his cheek. You weep for the poor, she said, for you yourself were once poor, and you know their sufferings. This makes you honorable and good. Do you think the other rich merchants care for the poor as you do? My father did not—he cursed them as a weight around his neck. My first husband did not care about them either—he never pulled his nose out of his tractates of Talmud long enough to notice that there was any poverty in this world. And do you think that *ganef*

Menachem cared that he was bankrupting the one righteous man among the town's wealthy householders, the one merchant whose heart bleeds for the beggars and the blind and the lame and who opens his purse wide to help them?

If you fall from the Count's favor and lose the leasehold, do you think he will stop harvesting the timber on his lands? Of course not—His Lordship needs the fee owed on the lease to pay for his pretty mistresses in Warsaw and gilded carriages and beautiful clothes. He will find himself another Jew to do what needs to be done—no doubt someone without your concern for the poor.

Zalman responded meekly that he supposed the poor would be better off with him keeping the leasehold on the timber rights.

Exactly, Raizel continued. So if you truly care about the welfare of the poor, you will discreetly borrow the necessary sum from the community funds, and then you will pay it all back once our profits have resumed again—you can then toss in even more ducats if you wish.

Suppose you had been in this predicament *before* you had made your generous contribution for the upkeep of the poor. Well, in that case you would have delayed your contribution, right? Because first you would have paid your debt to the *Pan*, and only later, when your funds were replenished, would you have made your contribution to the community welfare fund.

How is what I am suggesting any different? This is the same as making a delayed contribution, after your affairs have been put back in order.

Zalman could think of no arguments to offer in response. Stealing from the community funds still seemed wrong, but he no longer understood why—Raizel had made the theft, or the borrowing, appear to him to be the only course of action to defend the poor and alleviate their suffering. He now felt a strange obligation to steal, or borrow, the necessary funds, although he also felt guilty about doing so.

Well? Raizel asked him. Will you do what must be done?

Zalman squeaked out a barely audible reply: Yes, I will.

The next morning, after prayers, Zalman told the *shammes* (beadle) of the synagogue that he needed to withdraw certain large sums from the community welfare fund for the dowries and trousseaus of several orphan brides spread about the outlying villages. The *shammes* looked suspicious—how could there be so many orphan girls in such tiny villages getting married all at once? Who had ever heard of so many *simchas* happening at the same time?

Zalman said he had been surprised too, but he had received a letter the previous night that had brought tidings of this great miracle—and how could he refuse the request for help? Wasn't this why the community raised these funds in the first place?

The *shammes* still appeared to be uncomfortable, and so he tried a different tack: To release the funds, he would need the names of the brides and their villages.

Zalman replied that he would send a messenger with the names and the villages.

With that, Zalman walked away. Two hours later, he dispatched a servant with a list of various made-up names of brides and villages. The servant promptly returned with the requested funds in hand.

Zalman then rode out in his carriage to the Count's manor house, where he paid the balance owing on the lease fee to His Lordship's estate manager.

IV. The Temptation and Fall of the Most Noble Count Jan P.

WITH MENACHEM GONE, Zalman's profits swelled once more. As soon as he was able, he gave generously again to the community welfare fund—gave back far more than he had taken. He said to himself: The Holy One, Blessed be He, works in wondrous ways. While I worried that I was stealing, I was actually furthering His desire that there be even more money given to charity—this terrible situation could not have ended so well unless this had been His intention all along.

But then one evening, at twilight, there was a knock at Zalman's door. The Count's steward, with a panicked look on his face, told Zalman that His Lordship, Count Jan P., had just returned from an extended stay in Vienna and demanded that Zalman travel immediately to his manor house for a private audience. The carriage and coachman were waiting outside—he must leave with them at once.

Zalman turned to his Raizel, his expression imploring her to tell him what to do. But she looked away from Zalman and smiled warmly at the steward. Of course, she said, but first, please give me a moment to pack a parcel of food for my husband. We would not want to trouble the *Pan* with having to send for kosher food in the middle of the night.

Zalman followed her into the kitchen. As she packed kugel, bread, cheese, and a flask of kosher wine, she spoke to him sharply in a hushed tone: Whatever you do, do not anger the *Pan*. Flatter him, humor him, agree with him. He is probably drunk and wants either to weep or to rage. Either way, make sure you do not lose his affection and esteem.

Then she shoved the parcel into his hands and pushed him back towards the steward, who in turn grabbed his arm and pulled him into the coach, so that, before Zalman had entirely grasped what was happening, he found himself on a soft cushion in a huge carriage racing past the wheat fields on the bumpy road to the manor house of Count Jan P., lord of those lands.

By the time the carriage had pulled up to the manor house, the sky had grown dark, and a sliver of a moon had risen. The Count's steward grabbed Zalman's arm again and pulled his trembling body up the steps to the veranda, past the marble columns, and through the tall dark doors.

Once inside, Zalman was dazzled by the brightness of the many candles burning in the chandeliers. He turned his eyes to one of the walls, where he saw a fresco of beautiful men and women in skimpy tunics riding on pink clouds in dramatic poses.

He then felt the steward pull his arm once more and drag him at dizzying speed through a labyrinth of winding hallways, occasionally bumping into distracted and angry servants carrying pots or linens, until they reached a small room lit only by the moonbeams shining through a bay window. The steward pushed Zalman down into a lushly upholstered chair and walked away.

For several agonizing minutes, everything was silent and still in the dark room.

And then the door opened again. A tall, beautifully dressed man came in holding a candle that illuminated his clean-shaven face and prominent brow. This must be His Lordship, Zalman thought, and he tried to rise in respectful greeting, but he had fallen so deeply into the soft cushion of the chair that he only succeeded in rolling over to the side.

The *Pan* sat down on a chair opposite him and placed the candle on a small round table. He smiled indulgently at Zalman's bungled greeting and then leaned back and sighed. Zalman's terror now reached a fever pitch: He had no idea what a nobleman would expect of him or why he had been corralled so urgently and forcefully into this meeting. He offered a silent prayer to the Holy One, Blessed be He, for safe passage through this ordeal.

And then, to Zalman's relief, the Count addressed him:

My dear Zalman, thank you for visiting me upon such short notice. I knew your wife's father for many years, a fine man, a credit to your people. His death was a terrible tragedy. I wish I had been able to attend both his funeral and your wedding to his charming daughter. So I now offer you my belated condolences and my belated congratulations.

Zalman quickly and politely thanked him.

Now you must be wondering, the Count continued, why I have asked you to come here tonight. Do not worry, I mean you no harm. I welcome you to my house as a loyal friend and an honored guest. No, as more than a loyal friend: as a trusted confidante, a man who can guard secrets and follow through on delicate matters that must, of their very nature, remain discreet. Your wife's father was such a man—I have never met anyone more trustworthy, more faithful than he was, God rest his soul. Will you swear to me now, on whatever is holy to you Jews, that you will be the same?

Zalman so swore without hesitation. But his heart was heavy with worry—what could this lord possibly want him to do that had to be kept so secret?

Good, the Count resumed. I knew that Raizel would not marry a man unless he was every bit as wise and steadfast as her beloved father had been. What I must tell you, and what you must do, cannot be spoken of ever again.

As I said, I was not able to attend your wedding because I have long been away from my estates. I had first traveled to Warsaw. My daughter, my Karolina, was in the flower of her youth and beauty. Since her mother had passed on to the next world several years ago, it fell to me to introduce her to society and to eligible young suitors.

But after her first ball—and she was so radiant that night, like an angel who had drifted down from heaven—she took suddenly ill. She burned with fever for weeks, but even the finest physicians were of no avail. Her sweet soul departed from this life.

I was devastated. All my joy burned to ashes on that deathbed. There would be no wedding to a gallant young man from a distinguished family and no grandson to inherit my lands and titles.

I could not bear to remain in Warsaw any longer. Every room in my residence there reminded me of Karolina. She had given off a unique smell—like lavender, but stronger—it must have been some perfume she wore too heavily—that smell was now everywhere I turned in Warsaw and I felt my throat twist and choke as I inhaled it. I had to leave.

But I could not return here—I was sure that lavender scent would also creep out of the crevices of this manor house where she had slept for so many nights. No, I had to go somewhere new, some place where Karolina had never been.

So I ordered my coachman to make for Vienna. Why Vienna? I cannot say. Perhaps it was fate—an ugly fate hatched by the Devil himself to twist his sharp talons deep into my ribs. The Devil's servants certainly slithered merrily through that wretched city.

When I arrived, I took a fine suite of rooms at an elegant inn. The oily, fat innkeeper irritated me with his obsequious manner, but the accommodations were comfortable, and his cook was excellent—those warm apple strudels are my only happy memory of that cursed Vienna.

I knew no one there. Her Majesty the Empress Maria Theresa was not about to receive me, nor could I expect to be invited to any glittering affairs of Austrian society, which was fine with me. I needed to be alone if I hoped to calm the turmoil in my soul. I took long walks at night, brooding on the injustice of my daughter's death, my wife's death, all the misery in the world.

I discovered an old bridge where I would stand very still and listen to the Danube rush beneath me. I thought of how much death the river had seen and forgotten—how absurd was my trifling grief to the mighty Danube which had drowned Roman soldiers and Christian knights and Turkish janissaries.

Oftentimes I would lean my head over the edge of the railing and watch the dark water flowing in the pale moonlight.

One evening I must have shown my despair all too clearly because a stranger approached and pleaded with me not to jump off the bridge—it is a sin, he said, don't let your immortal soul be damned as a suicide. And life still has its pleasures—whatever ails your heart, it shall pass.

Truth be told, I had not considered jumping into the river. But nevertheless, it was good to hear a sympathetic voice. I could tell from his speech that the stranger was high born: He spoke that impeccable, precise French that only the most refined governess can properly impart. And when I turned around to look at my would-be savior, he had a fine bearing and elegant clothes.

Thank you for your kind words, I replied in French. I have fled far from my home, in grief over my daughter's death, to this distant city, where I know no one.

But now you know me, he said. Come, let us taste some sweet pleasure tonight—you can have a brief respite from your sadness.

He took me by the hand and led me away from the bridge and through several dark alleyways where I could easily have been stabbed, robbed, or worse. I should have been scared, but I was somehow fearless, as if everything in Vienna were not real but a fevered dream.

Eventually, we stopped at a narrow door with a big brass knob in the shape of a wolf. My new friend knocked, a head popped out, he gave the password, and we were permitted entrance. We then walked into a brightly lit room filled with finely dressed men and women and the sounds of softly joyful music.

My new friend introduced me to a woman and told her that I was in need of a kind lady to dance with me and ease my sorrows. She laughed and grabbed my hand and soon I was dancing, dancing as if I was again a young gallant in Warsaw.

Her name was Luisa. She was a Spaniard, and ravishing with her huge black eyes. I could tell she was not young, but neither did she appear to be old. She seemed to exist outside of ordinary time, like a creature from an enchanted realm who was a guest for the night in our human world.

After we had exhausted ourselves dancing, Luisa and I rested together on a couch. I had lost track of my new friend—he had vanished into the air just as suddenly as he had appeared on the bridge all those hours earlier. But I was so enamored of Luisa that I did not care. We drank sweet Hungarian wine and laughed, and it was wonderful—the burden of grief was lifted from my heart, and I was floating in the air like a droplet of mist.

Then the window curtains were opened wide, letting in the harsh light of the dawn. Our host, whomever he was, had signaled that it was time for us all to leave. I offered to escort Luisa back to her lodgings, but she refused. Instead she asked me to take her back to *my* lodgings. I should have been suspicious—something was clearly not right—but I had been so happy drinking in Luisa's dark, intense beauty that I seized this opportunity to keep her in my company.

We rode in a hired carriage back to my inn. There, Luisa and I spent a glorious day in bed: We slept, we embraced, we kissed, we became lovers. We drank port and nibbled on sweetmeats. She told me that she loved me and never wanted to leave my side. With my head spinning like a foolish boy, I agreed that she could stay in my rooms however long she wished. I sent my servants to her lodgings to fetch her things and I paid a bit extra to the innkeeper not to complain about my keeping a mistress.

The next few days were among the happiest of my life. There is a phrase in Latin I learned from my tutors when I was a little boy—*Et ego in Arcadia*, I too in Arcadia, in the peaceful, perfect forests and meadows of the ancient poets. Those days in Vienna, in Luisa's arms, were my Arcadia.

I especially loved the mornings. No matter how late in the night we had stayed awake, she would always rise at dawn. Her rustling would wake me too, but I pretended to still be asleep, so I could watch her without being noticed. She would walk from the bed to the tall mirror leaning against the wall, remove her night-gown, and stand there naked, examining herself. She made all sorts of odd expressions as she looked at now one part of her flesh and then another. She seemed strangely dissatisfied, as if her body were a dress that the tailor had not stitched together quite correctly. But to my eyes, she was the goddess of love incarnate: her olive skin, her raven hair, the grace with which she pivoted her feet ever so slightly and shifted her weight—with every look, I fell more deeply in love.

I unburdened my heart to Luisa, and I wept bitter tears for my daughter. Luisa comforted me and said that Karolina was now with her Heavenly Father. When she whispered these words into my ears, and held me tightly, the warmth of her embrace would run through my whole body and my pain would ease.

She also unburdened her heart to me. Her family, she said, was from Spain, near Cordoba. Her father had been a proud man, the scion of a long noble line. She had spent her childhood in a high stone tower, like a princess in an old romance, dreaming of the handsome cavalier who she would one day marry.

But then her father died. Unbeknownst to his family, he had incurred considerable debts, and their estates were mortgaged several times over. Creditors now demanded either their money or their collateral, the family's ancient lands. Horrified that these vultures would dare to threaten to dispossess a family of the noblest and purest blood, her mother appealed to the crown for mercy and protection. But the royal magistrates, doubtless bribed by the unscrupulous moneylenders, said the law was the law and the contract was the contract; and they hardened their hearts to any pleas for Christian charity.

Luisa soon had even more reason to be scared. The chief creditor, an old man with a fat belly, had intimated that he would perhaps forgive the debt if he were given the lovely young Luisa's hand in marriage. The royal magistrates thought this was a fair trade, and the local bishop pressed the idea too. To her horror, Luisa watched her mother and brother seriously consider the proposal.

Perceiving no other means of escape from a marriage of certain misery, one evening, in the dead of night, Luisa packed a small valise, stole some money, and fled with two trusted servants. She smuggled herself over the border to France and from France made her way to Vienna. She told me that she had been forced to live humbly, often relying upon the charity of good, pious Christians.

Now, she said, if only you, my beloved, could advance me the money to redeem my family's estates, we could marry and live in my beautiful palace in the Spanish countryside.

How much do you need? I asked.

The sum she named was staggering. While you, my friend Zalman, may think me rich, I have never possessed wealth on that scale. Only the very grandest magnates in Poland or Lithuania could pay such a figure.

So I was compelled to admit that I lacked the necessary funds.

Nevertheless, she pressed me further: But you do, though, dearest Jan, have money to stake at the card games played by the nobles? Could you not win enough to obtain the money I need? Please, my love?

And her eyes were full of desperate, pleading hope.

I told her that no man could win consistently enough to rack up the monies she was seeking. All gamblers lose more often than they win, I said, and hence I have always avoided the card tables as a fool's errand.

Now her expression changed—gone was the pleading; she smiled eagerly, and her eyes flamed with desire. But I can guarantee you will never lose, she said.

How is that? I asked.

And then she told me a truly bizarre tale. During her flight across France, she had met a monk, a Brother Raymond. This Brother Raymond had been defrocked for dabbling in dark magic. But he was not a bad man, she insisted, only a passionate seeker after knowledge, even from sources that the Church, with its prejudices, may frown upon. This Brother Raymond had traveled with her to Vienna, posing as her cousin, and he was staying at her lodgings in town.

Brother Raymond, she continued, had made an extraordinary discovery in the course of his occult investigations: he had deciphered the conjurations that ensured a player's victory at cards each and every time. Why don't you meet with him, Luisa cooed, and learn his secrets? Then you will never lose.

While I was moved by her speech—it is hard to resist the entreaties of a woman so beautiful, whom your heart naturally inclines to please and to protect—I still had some semblance of my wits left. If the monk had figured out how to always succeed at the card table, why hadn't he made himself rich long ago? Or why hadn't Luisa already used this knowledge to her benefit? There seemed to be no good reason to wait years and wander across countries just to find a melancholy Polish count to play cards on your behalf.

But she insisted that they had never before had access to the funds needed to stake themselves in a sufficiently lucrative game, with wealthy lords as the other players. And anyway Brother Raymond was of low birth—nobles would never accept him into their casinos.

Yet no doubt seeing the distrust lingering in my eyes, she tried a different approach: And besides, she continued, what is the harm in trying? Speak to Raymond, learn his method, and stake a small amount at a gambling table. If this is all a fraud, then you will lose only a very little.

This argument at last overcame my resistance—a small experiment could do no real harm. So I agreed to meet the fallen monk.

That night, Luisa led me to her lodgings, a modest house in a gloomy alley. We were greeted by an old woman who exchanged sharp words with Luisa in a language I did not know—Spanish, perhaps (she always spoke French with me). After they had finished their argument, whatever it was about, we went to a room in the back. Everything about the place was barren and ugly—peeling grey walls, dim smoky candles, rat droppings strewn about the floors—it was difficult to conceive how a flower as lovely as Luisa had continued to bloom in such a wasteland.

The monk, Brother Raymond, was seated at a wooden desk, hunched over a tome in Latin. In the weak candlelight I struggled to make out his withered and bony features.

After Luisa introduced me and stated our business, the monk, in a trembling, thin voice, explained how he had discovered, buried deep within a monastery library somewhere in Brittany, an ancient manuscript that examined how the Devil uses gambling to lure and tempt sinners. To break the Devil's grip on gamblers, the author had painstakingly laid out the dark magic employed by Lucifer to ensure that gamblers always lose in the end, thus driving them to desperate measures—robbery, murder, prostitution—to pay off their debts. It was this author's opinion that, if gamblers could win every time, then not only would these terrible consequences never come to pass, but the organizers of card games would soon be bankrupted and forced to abandon their vile labors. The manuscript concluded with an account of how the author had utilized his knowledge of necromancy to summon and interrogate a demonic spirit, whom he had compelled to reveal the secrets to guaranteed winnings at the card table.

Brother Raymond then revealed these secrets to me, made me repeat them several times to be sure I had committed them to memory and asked me to leave—he had already wasted too much time away from his studies, he said.

The next evening Luisa brought me to a sumptuous manor house just outside of Vienna where there was to be gambling all through the night. How she knew of this place, or the password to get in, I cannot say; in retrospect, many things seem hard to explain about those dreamy nights in Vienna.

Inside, the chandeliers reflected brightly against the pink walls and the tall mirrors. We sat down at a table and asked to play the next hand. I quickly ascertained that my fellow gamblers were the cream of Viennese society, great lords from Hungary, Bohemia,

Styria, there to try their luck as they whiled away their time in the Empress's court.

That night, I tested Brother Raymond's system. And it worked: I won every hand. I went from skeptic to enthusiast, and soon my heart pounded with anticipation at each new card that was drawn. The other players congratulated me on my skill and luck. The dealer eyed me suspiciously—he must have thought I was cheating somehow—but he could discover no trick.

After we had finished and were traveling back to our inn, I handed over all my winnings to Luisa, as an initial payment to her to reclaim her family's lands. When I reached my bed, I collapsed into a deep, satisfied sleep, dreaming of my future triumphs at the card table.

For the next three nights, my winning streak continued at the secret casino just outside the city. And I gallantly gave it all to her, the beautiful maiden to whom I had pledged my troth as a knight of the card games.

On the following night, though, Luisa said she was ill and could not accompany me. I no longer cared, however; I was only aroused by the thrill of winning. So I bid her an early good night and traveled to the casino alone.

But that evening, I lost every hand. I was sure that I was only erring in a small, but key, part of the occult formula and that once I had corrected myself, I would win it all back. And so I kept betting. I pledged estates, lands, houses, anything to stay in the game so I could taste sweet victory once more.

By the time the sun rose again, I was ruined.

I returned to my lodgings, crestfallen and ready to ask Luisa to give me back some of my prior winnings so I could pay off my new debts, just enough until I started to win again—and then I would more than repay her.

But when I arrived at my inn, Luisa was gone. The servants told me she had left for a stroll and never returned. I dispatched my valet to the house where I had met Brother Raymond, but he found it empty and said that there were no signs that anyone lived there.

The scales now fell from my eyes. I immediately packed my things, settled my bill with the innkeeper, and returned home to my estates in Poland.

My creditors are now hounding me without mercy. I owe them—and here the Count Jan P. named a staggering sum.

And so I turn to you, Zalman, for assistance in my hour of need. You are the wealthiest Jew on my lands; your wife's family has prospered greatly because of my favor. And I have always treated your family well. I never unfairly raised the lease payment or tried to bring in other Jews to outbid you. I let you make fair— no, more than fair—profits selling my timber. But now it is time for you to return my kindness. I need you to loan me the funds to pay off my debts. There is no one else to whom I can turn. My relatives and so-called friends would use this as an opportunity to seize my lands. And if word gets out as to what has happened, my good name will be in tatters.

Even though you are not a Christian, I know you are a good man, honest and upright, and that you will not hesitate to aid a man who is more than a lord to you—he is a genuine friend—a friend to you, to your family, and to all the Jews who live on my estates. Help me now and you will never lose your leasehold rights on the timber in my forests. I may even see fit to lease you the dis- tillery, too, and the toll collections and the fish ponds.

And your people will never know fear on my lands. I will drive away your persecutors and tolerate no slanders against my Jews. I will build you a new, grander synagogue and I will restore your sunken gravestones. We will be great friends, yes, great friends indeed, my Jews and me.

V. The Second Stumble Downwards

BY THE TIME His Lordship had finished speaking, the hour had grown quite late. A servant was rustled up, a bed was made, and soon an exhausted Zalman collapsed in sleep. In the morning, the steward woke him and brought him home to his Raizel.

She greeted him nervously and quickly led him into the bedroom. After carefully closing and bolting the door, she leaned in close and asked in a hushed voice: Is the *Pan* happy? Do we have his favor still?

Zalman pushed her away and sat down on a chair. He explained the situation as best he could: His Lordship was quite happy with them and overflowing with good feelings—too many good feelings. The *Pan* had been ruined by his gambling debts and now wanted a loan in the amount of—and he named the enormous sum—which they did not have, as they were still rebuilding their capital after Menachem's thieving. So what could they do? This was the end of them and their fortune.

Zalman slouched back and stared at the ceiling, wallowing in his despair. But then he suddenly felt a hard smack on his face. Startled, Zalman saw a furious Raizel hovering above him.

She said: Listen to me—we are not ruined. The *Pan* is not ruined. We will need another loan from the community's funds, that is all. This difficulty is, ultimately, the community's responsibility. The Count has been good to his Jews, and he has protected us. Should he lose his lands to these creditors, who knows what wicked persecutor, what new Haman or Titus, could take his place as our lord?

Zalman nodded. Then it is agreed, he said, tomorrow I shall summon the other trustees who oversee the community funds, and we will meet with the rabbi and craft a plan to raise the necessary funds for the *Pan*.

But at these words, Raizel's eyes again flared with rage. You fool, she said. The *Pan* believes we have the funds he needs. He wants to conceal his shameful circumstances. If you return with a loan from the community, he will think that you have betrayed him by spreading embarrassing details about his behavior—details that he trusted to tell you, and only you, as a friend. As soon as he has his hands on the money, he will exact his revenge for your betrayal by terminating our leasehold rights and expelling us from his lands.

And what will your fellow trustees think? They will smell your weakness—they will grasp that you have already lost your wife's great fortune. They will no longer defer to you; they will undermine you, strike new business alliances behind your back. And they will whisper about your fast depleting reserves of capital.

The merchants to whom we sell the timber will think you desperate and refuse to buy unless you drastically lower the prices, thereby ruining you—you will be forced to sell the logs for less than it costs to chop down the trees. No one is merciful to the weak.

This matter must be settled discreetly. Go in to inspect the community funds, remove the sum needed, and jot something down in the ledger—emergency expenditures for the care of the infirm in the far outlying villages. You did this sort of discreet borrowing once before—was it so terrible? Did anyone miss the money while it was gone? Did anyone complain? Of course not. You borrowed a bit, and then you repaid, with interest. Everything worked out for the best. So it will again.

Zalman wanted to object that this seemed more like stealing than borrowing, but to do so would have been to condemn himself for his own past behavior. He was not an evil man, he told himself, and nothing bad had happened the last time—just as Raizel had said, no one had missed the funds while they were, only temporarily, put to other uses. And he had scrupulously repaid each ducat and then some. These matters were confusing, but maybe that was the lot of the very rich—to have more difficult problems than ordinary men, requiring more difficult solutions.

Thus Zalman agreed to take out another secret loan from the community coffers. Raizel smiled sweetly at his words and smothered his face in hot, moist kisses.

That night, in the pitch-black early morning hours, Raizel woke Zalman and told him it was time to go out and take possession of the necessary funds. He hurriedly dressed and walked to the *bet midrash*, where the community funds and ledger were kept. He crept along as silently as he could, terrified that his loud breathing would wake the whole town and expose him as a thief.

Zalman entered the *bet midrash* with his small lantern, walked past the vestibule, and then off to the side, where he found the stairs leading to the upstairs floor. There, he groped about until he found the right door, which he unlocked with the special key that had been handed over to him as a trustee of the community funds.

Once inside, he rapidly counted out the necessary sum and stuffed the money into his purse. Then he reached for the ledger book. Zalman knew that he needed to doctor several entries to cover the large withdrawal, but his mind went suddenly blank. His temples throbbed and his stomach twisted with pain and nausea. He was terrified—without the false entries to cover up what he was doing, the theft would be obvious, he would be discovered, condemned, shamed—but still, he could not focus clearly enough to think through what he needed to write down.

In his desperation, he started writing down various figures, in amounts that he hoped would add up to the correct sum, but he was not sure, his head was dizzy, and the Hebrew letters were dancing about. But he had to write something, yes, something in the ledgers was better than nothing, scribble now, fast, while the town still slept. For all he knew someone might examine everything the very next morning.

On and on his hand went in a mad frenzy until there was a mess of zigzagging new withdrawal entries in the ledger with cryptic, one-word explanations—dowry, blind, dowry, cripple, orphan, cripple, dowry, etc.

When he decided that he had written enough, he rushed back home. He did not breathe easily again until he had returned to the manor house the next morning and provided the necessary sum to His Lordship.

VI. A Corpse in the River

ZALMAN SLEPT EASILY for the next few weeks, dreaming merrily of the many favors he was sure the Count would now lavish upon him. His love for Raizel swelled: Every movement of her body seemed so graceful, and her face was so lovely, even when she frowned in frustration at some inept servant. And she no longer criticized her husband: All his actions were clever and bold in her telling, and she indulged every one of his whims and appetites, from warm honey cakes to fine Hungarian wines to the pleasures of the flesh.

But then one morning, as he was finishing his prayers in the synagogue, the *shammes* (beadle) approached and asked to have a word in private. Zalman felt an anxious chill shoot through his bones. Ever since the *shammes* had doubted Zalman's excuses for his first theft—or borrowing—of community funds, Zalman had taken pains to avoid his company.

The *shammes* led him to a dark, secluded alcove in the back of the building. Yet after they were alone, the *shammes* fell silent and stared at his feet. Once or twice sounds began to pass from his lips, but they quickly dissolved in the air without forming into words.

Zalman finally broke the impasse: *Nu?* You wanted to speak to me. Well, here we are, so speak and be done with it. I have business to attend to.

The *shammes* now looked up into Zalman's eyes. Zalman thought there was something sad and searching in his gaze, as if the *shammes* were trying to find a precious item that had been lost.

And then the *shammes* spoke: It gives me no pleasure to say this. You are a respected man, and a wealthy man, but you act in sinful ways. I will never understand why Raizel married you and raised you to such heights in this world. If her father of blessed memory were still amongst us, this match would never have happened.

Zalman felt his rage start to simmer. Who was this lowly functionary, a man who cleaned the lamps and the candlesticks in the synagogue, to look down his nose at the town's greatest merchant, the secret confidante of a mighty Polish lord? Was it not Zalman's generosity that provided the funds to pay the salary of this sanctimonious beggar?

But before Zalman could give vent to his fury, the *shammes* spoke again: Yesterday, funds were requested to repair the ritual bath—the ceiling beams have been rotting for some time and the storm from the other day made everything much worse. So it was clear the bath house needed to be repaired. Yes, it needed to be repaired.

And then he paused again and breathed hard.

Zalman could no longer stand this silly dithering: So, the ritual bath has to be repaired, fine, go ahead and repair it. What has this to do with me? Why must I stand here all day in this dark corner listening to your babbling? Say what you actually want to say or leave me in peace.

The *shammes* now straightened his back and responded in a forceful tone: Fine, I will say what I must say. When I learned of the needed repairs, I consulted the records of the community's accounts, to make sure there was sufficient money in hand. And what did my eyes see in those ledgers? Mad, zigzagging numbers and stray words like cripple and blind and dowry. When I unlocked the chest where the coins are kept, I found a substantial sum was gone, similar to—but not the exact amount of—the scrawl in the ledger.

Then the *shammes* fell silent again and looked at Zalman with smug, judging eyes, as if, Zalman thought, he was awaiting a tearful confession from a naughty child. Of course, Zalman did know he was guilty. But how could the *shammes* have known what he had done? The *shammes* must have assumed that any irregularity in the accounts was evidence of the wicked greed of the artisan who had married too far above his station and needed to be pulled back down to his proper place.

Feeling enraged once more, Zalman snapped back harshly in reply: But what does this have to do with me? You obviously failed to safeguard the community's funds. You will have to answer for your own incompetence.

The *shammes* sighed again—the sound of that sigh felt to Zalman like a sharp needle being driven into his temple—and spoke: Very few men have keys to enter the room where these monies are kept. And of those very few men, you are the only one whom I have seen make large withdrawals to benefit a multitude of poor brides whose names I did not recognize.

I found the promissory note you had written earlier in the year for a sum to be drawn upon by the community. I compared the handwriting: the same clumsy, crooked letters of an *am haaretz*, an ignorant, uneducated man. Who else could it be but you? Your fellow trustees are learned men, scholars who in their youth had studied at distinguished *yeshivot*.

Zalman suddenly felt his chest tighten painfully. He wanted to shout out that this was nonsense, but he could not utter a sound.

The *shammes* went on: I have no desire to shame you. Return the money and step down as a trustee of community funds. You can say that you are too preoccupied with your business affairs.

Zalman once more tried to speak but could not push his words past his trembling lips. Feeling dizzy and confused, he said nothing and quickly stumbled away from the dark alcove. He left the synagogue.

Throughout the rest of that morning, the pains in Zalman's chest grew steadily worse and there was a pounding in his forehead as if a hail of stones were being hurled against his head. Finally, he stood up from his desk, but then immediately fell unconscious onto the floor.

When he awoke again, he was lying in his bed, alone except for Raizel standing over him. He felt hot and sore, and there was dried sweat sticking to his skin.

At the sight of his wife's soft, loving eyes, and feeling the gentle way she applied a towel to his forehead, Zalman burst into tears of tenderness. Thinking back to his conversation with the *shammes*, he trembled as he pondered the shame he had brought upon Raizel through his sinful actions. True, she had urged him to do the theft, but it was still his doing—and what husband does every foolish thing his wife suggests?

Pulling himself upright, Zalman told Raizel that he had important news to share. He then described, in a halting voice, how the *shammes* had uncovered his newest theft from the community funds.

We are ruined, he said to her. He wants the money returned now, but it will be some time before the *Pan* can repay us or our profits will be sufficiently large again. I must leave, go somewhere where I am not known. No, first I will give you a divorce so you can remarry—to a distinguished scholar, wise and good, not like me, no, this marriage was madness—you belong with a scholar whose learning and saintliness matches your beauty. You can be happy again, and I shall atone for my many sins by begging for my bread and sleeping naked in the snow.

But Raizel responded in a warm voice: My sweet husband, what is this nonsense about divorce and running away? You are my *bashert*, the one whom I have been destined to marry since my soul entered this world. This is what was revealed to me by the holy Rabbi Israel ben Eliezer, the Baal Shem Tov, pillar of our generation, may his merit protect us from all harm. To undo a match like ours, a match made by the angels themselves in the Heavenly Court, would be a terrible sin.

So, the *shammes* turned his ugly wrinkled nose up at you? He is a weak old man, a nuisance. Do not worry yourself about this matter anymore. You are ill and you must rest. I will see to it that the *shammes* ceases to trouble you.

Raizel then placed her fingers over his eyelids and slowly closed them. Soon the warm embrace of sleep overcame him.

And then Zalman had the strangest dream: He beheld a circle of women holding hands and dancing around a tree in the moonlight. Raizel was there, but he did not recognize the others. They were beautiful, though, with blonde hair, pale faces, and the immodest, low-cut dresses favored by noblewomen. They were singing a song, but there was something harsh and spiteful in the tune. The circle moved faster and faster, and the ground groaned—yes, actually groaned, he heard it—but Raizel looked down, smirked, and spat upon it.

Zalman wanted to tell her not to be so cruel—be kind to the ground, he thought, it is suffering beneath your feet, you and your friends are pounding so hard upon it. But he could not speak. In anguish and frustration his eyes opened, and he sat up in his bed.

He was alone and the room was dark, except for a sliver of white moonlight creeping in through the curtains. He rose with difficulty—his body was stiff—and walked gingerly to the window.

He opened it up and leaned outside. An easy, cool breeze massaged his face in the quiet night.

But then he heard a faint rustling and looked over to his left. He saw a tall tree. Beneath it was a group of women holding red candles in their hands. Raizel was in the group, but he did not recognize the others, although, just like in his dream, they were blonde and wore immodest, low-cut dresses.

Raizel led the group of strange women away from Zalman's house. They soon turned into an alleyway, and he lost sight of them. Drowsiness overcame him once more and, unsure if he was still dreaming, Zalman stumbled back into bed and fell into a deep sleep.

The next morning his body again felt strong and healthy. He was still not sure what to do about the *shammes*, but he decided to take a solitary walk after morning prayers to help clear his mind. Once he had put his thoughts into proper order, he would speak again with Raizel.

At the synagogue that morning, he noticed that the other householders appeared uneasy. Zalman leaned over to the man next to him and asked what had happened—had someone fallen ill or died during the night? Had there been a fire?

In response, the man pointed his finger toward a back corner in the synagogue. There, Zalman saw the *shammes*. But he was no longer the confidently accusing man of the day before. He now looked feverish and trembling, with tears gushing down his face and his eyes darting madly about, as if he felt in terrible danger from some hidden menace about to leap out at him from the shadows.

Zalman was baffled. What could have happened? But before he could muster the courage to approach closer, the *shammes* packed up his *tallis* and *tfillin* in a small velvet bag and ran out of the synagogue in a mad panic, as if being chased by a pack of vicious dogs.

Zalman quickly finished his prayers and left to attend to his affairs. He tried not to think any more about the *shammes*.

At twilight that same day, there was a loud commotion outside Zalman's offices, with a great deal of wailing and weeping. Unsure what was happening, he sent a servant into the crowd to find out more. In the meantime, he poured himself a glass of brandy and breathed heavily. He feared he was somehow implicated in whatever ill news was driving the Jews into turmoil, although he reminded himself to be careful—he did not know yet what exactly was being said in the town square.

His servant returned a quarter of an hour later with a gruesome tale: The *shammes* had been found dead, his naked body floating in the river. His wrists had been cut open and there was blood everywhere in the water. All that day the *shammes* had acted strangely, trembling, weeping, and, when anyone tried to comfort him, insisting he was the vilest sinner, a sick, evil man who merited no kindness and no mercy.

He had babbled on about needing to wash away the sin smeared all over his skin and so he had gone down to the river.

The last words anyone had heard the *shammes* speak were a garbled quote from the Prophet Jeremiah: Though you wash with soap and lye, and rub and rub, your guilt is marked before Him, the Holy One, Blessed be He.

Later that evening, Zalman spoke to Raizel about the *shammes*. He told her that he felt somehow responsible—that whatever evil spirit had tormented the *shammes* was connected in some way to his own sin in stealing from community funds.

Raizel stared at him quietly for a moment and then burst out laughing. When she had recovered herself again, she said: Oh my dear, foolish husband, why are you sad? You should rejoice—your persecutor, your very own personal wrinkled little Haman, has departed from this world. Dance and sing—the righteous of Israel have been delivered once more.

A terrible thought now arose in Zalman's mind and flew past his lips: *Raizel, did you have a part in what happened to the shammes?*

But she did not answer.

VII. Pilgrimage

THAT NIGHT, ZALMAN reflected upon his many sins. He was a thief who had stolen from community funds intended for the poor. He had used some of these stolen ducats to pay the debts of a Gentile lord who had squandered his fortune in foreign lands with gambling, black magic, and debauchery. And now he felt sure that he was guilty, in some way he could not fully discern, for the humiliation and death of the *shammes*.

Why had he committed these crimes? Because of his Raizel's twisted words and wicked counsel. Before his marriage, he had been poor and despised, but he had lived honestly and uprightly. Not that he had given his deeds too much thought back then—it had just never occurred to him to act in any other way.

Nor had he schemed for Raizel's hand. The thought of marrying her had never crossed his mind until *she* had approached *him* and insisted upon the match.

And why did this sinful woman, with a tongue like the serpent in *Gan Eden*, choose him of all people? Because a holy *tzaddik*, Rabbi Israel ben Eliezer, the Baal Shem Tov, had told her that he, Zalman, was her *bashert*, her destined bridegroom.

So that was the true cause of his suffering and his shame: the words of the holy saint, the Baal Shem Tov. Had this *tzaddik* chosen to tell her to marry somebody else—say, any one of the many rich *yeshiva bochurs* pining for her hand—then none of this would have happened to him.

Zalman thus concluded that the only way he could figure out how to atone for his sins and find his way back to a path of righteousness was to confront the Baal Shem Tov and find out why, exactly, he had been matched to such a monstrous demon of a wife.

And so the next morning Zalman filled up his purse with coins and rode off in his carriage to visit the Baal Shem Tov in the town of Mezhbizh.

He did not tell Raizel where he was going, but instead left word for her that he was traveling to various merchants to settle certain unspecified business affairs.

Upon his arrival in Mezhbizh after an uneventful journey, Zalman sent his coachman with a gift of money and a request for a meeting to the home of Rabbi Israel ben Eliezer, the Baal Shem Tov. He was not sure how easy it would be to gain entry into the saint's presence—when Jews told tales of the wonders of the Baal Shem Tov, they often praised his love for the poor and his scorn for the arrogant rich.

But it turned out that the *tzaddik* was not so averse to the company of rich men: Rabbi Israel ben Eliezer promptly invited Zalman to come and unburden his heart of whatever was weighing it down. And the Baal Shem Tov's house turned out to be no thatched hut in the forest—another fable spread by foolish tongues—but rather an elegant structure on the outskirts of town, where a slender but imposing man standing on the veranda warmly greeted Zalman.

This man introduced himself as Rabbi Alexander, scribe and secretary to Rabbi Israel ben Eliezer, and he flattered Zalman as shamelessly as any innkeeper's wife, praising his handsomeness and piety and plying him with brandy and honey cakes. After several minutes of such pleasantries, Rabbi Alexander excused himself to announce the esteemed and distinguished visitor to the Baal Shem Tov.

Rabbi Alexander returned a quarter of an hour later and conducted Zalman to a study in the back of the house. The room was dark and stuffy. Even though it was a pleasant sunny day, the thick red curtains had been drawn tightly, and the only light came from a smoky candle.

Although the room held surprisingly few books, there were amulets everywhere—piles and piles of them, heaped up on desks and chairs, as if Rabbi Israel ben Eliezer had been condemned by some bizarre judgment of the Heavenly Court to do nothing all day but write out amulets. These amulets had headings such as Childbirth, Sickness, Riches, Barrenness, and Beauty.

The Baal Shem Tov himself was short and big nosed, with the ugliest, patchiest beard that Zalman had ever seen—as if in his boredom and frustration at being compelled to write so many amulets he had torn out huge chunks of his beard to relieve his misery.

After Rabbi Alexander had made a polite introduction and exited, the Baal Shem Tov invited Zalman to sit down on a soft chair. Once Zalman had made himself comfortable, the *tzaddik* walked over to him and began sniffing his guest all over his body.

Once this sniffing was done, the Baal Shem Tov stood directly over Zalman's head and glared down into his eyes for several minutes. Zalman grew increasingly ill at ease. He felt as if he was being judged, and harshly, even though the Baal Shem Tov had not spoken a word.

But then Rabbi Israel ben Eliezer suddenly jumped away from his guest and ran to the other side of the room, knocking over several piles of amulets in his path. He doubled over in front of a closed curtain and fell to his knees. And then the mighty *tzaddik*, pillar of his generation, vomited. Yet this was no ordinary nausea, like a blacksmith or a coachman after a long night of drinking. Rather, Zalman was astonished to see that the Baal Shem Tov retched up a strange mixture of garishly bright red blood and a sticky black substance that smelled so horrible that Zalman himself felt queasy.

The sound of the vomiting was as loud as a thunderclap, and Rabbi Alexander, accompanied by some other men—disciples? servants?—whom Zalman had never seen before, burst in through the closed doors. They helped the Baal Shem Tov back up to his feet again and cleaned the gross liquids from his holy person.

Master, what has happened? Rabbi Alexander asked.

You brought me a soul that is rancid, Rabbi Israel said. Send him away for now, and I will speak with him again tomorrow morning, after I have recited the correct combination of holy names to fortify myself against his soul's stench and rot.

Before Zalman could say anything in reply, he was yanked violently out of the study, dragged past the parlor and across the veranda, and sent back to the inn where his coachman had stabled the horses.

Stupefied and exhausted, Zalman retired to his bed and stared at the ceiling until his eyes closed and sleep overwhelmed him.

VIII. Revelations and Judgments

EARLY THE NEXT morning, Rabbi Alexander approached Zalman during morning prayers in the synagogue and said that the holy *tzaddik*, Rabbi Israel ben Eliezer, the Baal Shem Tov, now wished to speak with him again. Still unnerved from the previous day's bizarre audience, Zalman hesitated at first, but Rabbi Alexander insisted—he must come at once, there could be no delay.

So Zalman meekly followed Rabbi Alexander back to the elegant house on the outskirts of the town, and once more into the study of the Baal Shem Tov. This time Rabbi Israel appeared composed and calm and did not engage in any more sniffing or staring. He smiled slightly and asked Rabbi Alexander to leave the two of them alone, as they had much to discuss.

After Rabbi Alexander had left, the Baal Shem Tov invited Zalman to sit down in the same chair again and gently asked what had brought such a distinguished man, such a wealthy merchant, to his poor and humble home?

Zalman breathed deeply and looked at the floor. Then he spoke:

Rabbi Israel, holy Baal Shem Tov, I am lost, and I need your guidance. I thought that I had been blessed with a miracle—I, a poor, ignorant blacksmith, had married the wealthiest and the most beautiful woman in my town, my wife Raizel. But then she led me into terrible sins—her cunning, deceitful tongue convinced me to discharge my debts by stealing from community funds for the poor and the infirm. When the *shammes* of our synagogue discovered my theft and demanded I make restitution, she told me not to worry. That night, I had a dream, or a vision, or maybe I saw, I don't know, I was in such confusion, but Raizel was wandering in the night with a pack of Gentile women wearing immodest dresses. And the next day, the *shammes* killed himself because something horrible and shameful had happened the night before—and my Raizel, she smiled and laughed at the news of this calamity.

At that moment, I finally grasped that my marriage was no miracle, but a horrible curse—that I was wed to a demon of some kind. And how had this disaster come to pass? When I had asked Raizel on our wedding night why she had chosen me and not some wealthy scholar with a distinguished lineage, she said that *you* had told her to wed me—that you, holy *tzaddik*, had revealed to her that I alone was her *bashert*, her destined one.

So tell me, did you say to Raizel that she must marry me? And if you did, why would you curse me this way?

Zalman now looked up again. The Baal Shem Tov was nodding his head slightly and let out a soft sigh. He slouched back in his chair, scratched his patchy beard, and responded in a firm voice:

Reb Zalman, your wife Raizel is your destined match. I revealed that truth to her when she came to me, and I tell it to you now that you are sitting here. But you ask me, how can this be? What have I done to merit such a fate?

The difficulty is that you do not comprehend the root of your soul and what it has done in its previous incarnations in this world. When your mother gave birth to your body in this life, your soul was already bathed in filth, putrid and disgusting to those who can perceive the true reality concealed beneath the surface of the things of this world of lies and illusion.

But let me begin at the proper beginning, which is with Raizel, not you. Raizel's soul also lived before, in other bodily husks. In a former incarnation, she was the daughter of a pious scholar and his modest wife. She had a twin brother, who was a prodigy, a genius, in the study of the Talmud. A good life had been decreed for her: She would marry a scholar like her father and her brother and raise fine sons who would love and cherish the Torah and all of its commandments. When she would eventually depart from this world, her praiseworthy sons and grandsons would study pages of the *Mishnah* in honor of her blessed memory, thereby elevating her soul to higher realms of purity.

But she chose not to walk in the path of the righteous. When she blossomed into a woman, a terrible pestilence swept the land—the liar and the fraud, may his name be cursed and forgotten, Sabbatai Zevi. This Sabbatai Zevi proclaimed himself to be the Messiah sent to redeem Israel. He had the arrogance to decree that, as the Messianic Age had supposedly dawned, laws and commandments were no longer to be heeded. Do you know what he would say, this evil piece of filth? He would shout in his loud voice, Blessed are You, Lord Our God, King of Universe, Who permits that which is forbidden.

On *Tishe Ba'Av*, when all decent Jews fast and weep for the destruction of the Temple in Jerusalem (may it be rebuilt speedily in our days), *he* ordered his disciples to celebrate with a great feast. And they obeyed him blindly because the fools had convinced themselves that this was the King Messiah himself commanding them—and who were they to question his holy wisdom?

And they were not alone. Jews from Poland to Holland to Italy to Turkey and beyond, all became convinced that this sinning fraud Sabbatai Zevi was the Messiah, come to redeem them from the sufferings of Israel's long and painful exile.

This belief in the deceiver, the false Messiah, also came to the town where Raizel's soul then resided. She began to have fits in the streets, screaming, foaming at the mouth, her arms and legs thrashing about, falling unconscious to the ground. And when she awoke, she was surrounded by a crowd gathered in concern for the afflicted girl. But then, to the crowd's amazement, she swore she had heard voices from Heaven, angels' voices, joyously proclaim that Sabbatai Zevi was the Messiah, sent at last to redeem Israel.

Her fits and visions seduced the hearts of the Jews in that town into sin and error, and they became fervent followers of the fraud, Sabbatai Zevi.

Alarmed at what was happening, Raizel's father—may the memory of the righteous be for a blessing—rose up and denounced his daughter's lies. He ordered her to behave with modesty and decency again and to stop making a ridiculous spectacle of herself in the streets.

But she had already fallen too far. She reveled in shamelessly flaunting herself before hushed, adoring crowds who hung on every word of her supposed visions of Sabbatai Zevi as Messiah. Rather than heed her wise father's harsh but just words, she denounced him to her followers as a heretic and a sinner who was working with the forces of darkness to thwart the mission of the Messiah. She cheered and sang, like Miriam with her tambourine, as she watched her supporters beat her father mercilessly and drive him away from the town.

With her father gone, *she* now reigned supreme, and spouted ever more outrageous prophecies—wild nonsense about the armies of the Lost Ten Tribes crossing the River Sambatyon to march under the banner of Sabbatai Zevi. She would denounce and persecute other Jews for insufficient zeal for the false Messiah and his mission. In her visions, she claimed to see secret plots being hatched against her Messiah, and she vowed to root them out by banishing any Jew who was an enemy of the wretched deceiver and hypocrite Sabbatai Zevi.

But then the Holy One, Blessed be He, decided that Israel had suffered enough. *HaShem* compelled the Sultan of Turkey to arrest Sabbatai Zevi and give him a choice: death or conversion to Islam.

Sabbatai Zevi, the supposed holy and powerful Messiah, immediately, without any hesitation, donned the turban and became a Muslim.

Once word spread of Sabbatai Zevi's cowardly betrayal, Jews finally abandoned the imposter and repented of their wicked ways. The householders in her town now realized that either Raizel had lied to them, or her visions had been sent by demons. This should have been the end of her—she should have been cast out and devoured by the Earth, like Korach—but, unfortunately, she was saved from the harsh fate she so richly deserved.

Her father, having now returned again to the town, was revered and exalted as a light unto his generation, who had seen through Sabbatai Zevi's lies all along and had boldly declared the truth, even at risk of his own life and safety. But he loved his daughter too much to see her punished for her wicked conduct, and he urged that she be pardoned, as she was only a young girl, clearly misled by others. His pleas won over the other householders, and she was permitted to live as freely as before.

But Raizel no longer wished to live a pious and upright life. *She* was still convinced of the truth of her visions that Sabbatai Zevi was the Messiah. While outwardly she acted as if she was a decent Jewish maiden, her soul was secretly in torment, trying to understand how the Messiah could have committed such an act of craven apostasy.

And then she met a traveling merchant who came to her town. He was a secret follower of Sabbatai Zevi who corresponded with other disciples of the false Messiah as far away as Salonica and

Constantinople. This man had heard rumors of the town's famous prophetess who had seen visions of Sabbatai Zevi and now he sought her out.

With cunning words, he quickly discerned that Raizel still believed in her prophecies. So he arranged to meet with her secretly at night, in the ruins of an abandoned hunting lodge deep inside a thick forest. There, the merchant revealed to Raizel the new and even more loathsome doctrines oozing out of the mouths of the remaining adherents of the deceiver, Sabbatai Zevi.

According to them, the so-called Messiah's conversion to Islam was not what everyone else thought it obviously was, that is, a clear sign that he was a liar and a hypocrite. No, to the contrary, this merchant maintained, Sabbatai Zevi was now pursuing his Messianic calling in a far more important and bold manner by abandoning the holiness of Israel and the Torah to enter into the Gentile world of demonic forces, the *kelipah*, where sparks of the light of the Holy One, Blessed be He, were trapped after being scattered and dispersed at the time of Creation. Sabbatai Zevi, according to this man, was hunting for these sparks trapped in the demonic realm and fighting to free and elevate them back to the Throne of Glory.

When the sun rose again, this traveling merchant slipped back to his inn, hitched his wagon, and drove off. Raizel would never see him again. But his words, so full of clever lies, had seized hold of her heart. She thought of nothing now but how the world could be saved only by delving into its worst, most heinous corners and rescuing the divine sparks trapped there. In her mind, there could be no redemption through the Torah and its commandments, as our sages of blessed memory had wisely taught. Instead, redemption could come only through sin.

As a prophetess of Sabbatai Zevi, she decided that she, too, must join in this sacred work of sinning to redeem the world. She considered baptism, to imitate her Messiah's apostasy, but she knew this would break her father's heart and she had just enough decency left not to inflict such a sorrow upon that righteous man in his old age.

So she resolved instead to sin amongst and with her fellow Jews. But what sins should she pick, as there are so many to choose from? She considered luring the town's householders into adultery; she was young and beautiful, after all, and their wives were not. But this seemed such a petty sin to her, the kind of transgression that is always humming about us, like flies in the summer. If the world is to be redeemed by sin, then the sins must be mighty enough to shake the ground beneath our feet.

She thought long and hard about what sin could truly be worthy of her great task, and she eventually decided to consult her women's Yiddish Bible. There, she came across the tale of Sodom and Gomorrah, cities which, in their time, had been unrivalled in sin. But she did not live in a great metropolis full of luxury and vice; her home was a modest *shtetl*, with its smattering of Jews and Poles and Ukrainians going about their simple business.

But Raizel read on. Our Father Abraham, may his merit protect us, had interceded with the Holy One, Blessed be He, to save his beloved nephew Lot from the destruction of Sodom. Lot's daughters, however, seeing fire rain down from the sky upon the wicked cities, were convinced that the world was being destroyed and that their father was the only man left alive. So they plied their father Lot with wine and, once he was drunk, they each lay with him as if he were their husband.

At last, this was the great sin which Raizel had been seeking. Still, she would not lie with her father—again, if she felt compassion for one Jewish soul, it was him. Instead, she turned her eyes towards her brother, the great Talmud prodigy.

One day, her father traveled away on business to a distant fair, where he would be gone for two or three weeks. Raizel purchased some vodka from the inn in town and, when her brother returned home, exhausted from a long day of studying in the town's *bet midrash*, she offered him the strong liquor to drink. She fawned over how wise and learned he was, how strenuously he parsed out the meanings of the most difficult, knotted words of the holy sages.

The foolish boy eagerly drank in both the vodka and the flattery. Eventually, he stumbled into his bed. By then, his drunken mind was spinning in circles, and he could no longer feel his own teeth.

Raizel snuffed out the candle in his room and then, after waiting for an hour to pass, she returned to her brother and joined him in his bed. In his drunkenness he did not understand, and saw only a beautiful woman, and felt only the pleasures of her flesh. She lay with him that night as Lot's daughters had lain with their father.

The next morning her brother was terribly ill, vomiting and moaning in pain from the pounding in his head. And it was not only his body which ached: His soul was in torment too. Tears flooded from his eyes, and he loudly denounced his own wickedness.

Raizel, pretending to be innocent, asked why he was so distraught. He replied that a woman had come in the night to his bed and he had sinned with her. But she told him it was only a bad dream, brought on by his sickness, as there was no strange woman who had entered their house the night before. Her words gave him comfort.

During the next three nights, Raizel again plied her brother with vodka and, once he was in a drunken stupor, again lay with him in his bed in the dark.

Soon her brother was trembling in terror. He thought that he had been afflicted for several nights in a row with the same evil dream of sinning in his bed with a mysterious woman. He was sure this could only be a demon attacking him, trying to distract him from his holy studies. Raizel, still feigning ignorance, agreed and urged him to seek aid and protection.

So her brother consulted several works of *Kabbalah* and found a formula for warding off demons. He carefully copied out the Hebrew incantation upon a piece of paper and tied it to a string necklace that he placed next to his heart.

That night he told Raizel about his new amulet and how he was hopeful that the demon would not be able to approach him again. In her cunning, she now served only weak wine and avoided his bed. When he awoke the next morning, healthy, untroubled in the night, he thought he had vanquished the demon and never suspected what had actually occurred.

But the terrible sin had already borne poisonous fruit: Raizel was with child. She hid her condition artfully, until it was time for her to give birth. Then she went into the woods, to the hut of a peasant woman who practiced black magic, where she gave birth aided by the all-evil powers in the world, may we be spared from such horrors.

That baby was you, Zalman—not in your current bodily incarnation, but the soul was the same one that is inside you now.

Raizel handed over the infant to a monastery just outside town. She had future plans for even greater sins with her incestuous bastard and did not want him to be raised as a Jew with knowledge of the holy Torah. She noted well a particularly telling birthmark of his, so she would be able to find him again in later years.

Now Raizel bided her time. Her father made a fine marriage match for her, to a distinguished and pious merchant. She had children with her lawful husband and acted as if she was a fine, righteous Jewish wife and mother.

She waited patiently for thirteen years until her bastard—that is, you—would be old enough to have seed of his own to make another child with her—a doubly incestuous bastard, a sin of such staggering heights that Raizel was sure the foundations of the universe would shake.

She saw you laboring in the monastery's garden, and recognized you by the birthmark on your left arm. She began to speak sweetly to you, to cajole and flatter you.

One day, she led you into a remote grove by a stream, and she kissed you as a bride kisses her groom.

But her scheme did not succeed. Shortly after that kiss, your former body was struck with a terrible fever, and in three days' time the Angel of Death harvested your soul.

Raizel collapsed into despair. Her great sin had been thwarted, and she had no opportunities for further crimes of this kind: her father had died, her brother had moved far away, and her children were girls. In her anguish, she determined upon what she felt was the highest sin still left open to her—suicide.

After she drank a long draught of poison, the avenging angels removed Raizel's soul from her body and flung it immediately into *gehenna*, the realm of the demons—for the Heavenly Court had no desire to waste its time judging the worth of such an obviously wicked soul.

In *gehenna*, Raizel sought out the soul of Sabbatai Zevi, which she found floating in a lake of burning sulfur. She hailed him as her King Messiah. He, in turn, acknowledged her as his disciple and prophet. But he rebuked her for not completing her terrible work of sinful redemption before her suicide. Her failure to descend deeply enough into sinfulness, he told her, had left holy sparks trapped in the realms of evil, and he ordered her to return to this world to complete her task.

Raizel's soul was now more determined than ever to consummate her great sin. She petitioned Ashmedai, king of the demons, to return her soul to this lowly world so she could bear a child with her incestuous bastard. Ashmedai was only too pleased with this suggestion. When the demon king learned that your soul was going to be reborn—the Heavenly Court had taken pity upon you, as your soul had been unjustly deprived of its chance to live as a Jew and earn merit by obeying the Torah's commandments—Ashmedai likewise released Raizel's soul to be reborn into a new body.

But when she reached the age to be married, Raizel now confronted a difficulty that she had not anticipated: You had been born into circumstances that made you an unsuitable match for her.

Ashmedai, who trades in the seductions and vanities of this world of illusion, had made sure that Raizel's soul would be reborn as a beautiful woman in a wealthy household.

The Heavenly Court, however, cares nothing for riches or physical beauty. The kind angels had merely wished for you to have the chance to live as a pious Jew following the Torah. After all, a simple blacksmith can pray with devotion, cleave to the Holy One, Blessed be He, with all his heart, and lead a life filled with small, but precious, *mitzvot*.

But Raizel was crafty. She rejected every match that her father offered to her, always finding some excuse or other. When her father visited me to seek my counsel, I saw clearly the putrid rot in his daughter's soul, and I knew that no man she married would live long—unless it were you. And thus I warned him: If your daughter should marry any man but Zalman the Blacksmith, her husband will quickly perish and there will be no children.

But her father scorned my words. He called me a madman and a fraud—he was wealthy, and his daughter was beautiful, so how could the match be anything but the best? Who ever heard of marrying a girl so pretty and so rich to an impoverished, dirty, ignorant smith?

And so he finally forced his daughter Raizel to marry a bridegroom who was learned, handsome, and wealthy. Yet Raizel's soul would not be diverted from its one true goal of completing her incestuous union with you. She now decided to free herself of every obstacle in her way: She poisoned both her husband and her father, so that she could become a wealthy widow free to pick her own husband.

How did a girl raised in a pious Jewish household, and married to a scholar devoted to the Talmud, acquire poison and know how to use it? From the wretched *Pan*, Count Jan P., who rules the lands where you live. She had met him through her father, who leased the Count's timber rights, and she took careful note of how the *goyische* lord's eyes followed her about the parlor in his manor house. She should have been ashamed, but instead she encouraged his attentions and arranged secret meetings, where she pleasured him in unnatural ways that cannot create a child. She sent other women to him, too, whom she called her ladies of the forest—demons, all of them, summoned from the burning tar pits of *gehenna* to do her bidding.

Once the *Pan* was smitten with her, Raizel begged him to supply her with poison—she swore that if she could only rid herself of her husband, she would visit her lover more often. The panting, overheated Count, sweating like a filthy pig beneath his wigs and powders and perfumes, his soul reduced to a plaything of his depraved fantasies, used his fortune and his retainers to get his mistress what she wanted.

But once the murders were accomplished, she counseled the *Pan* to flee abroad, so as to deflect suspicion.

Yet despite all these plots and crimes, *you* were not yet damned. She had freed herself to marry you, but you had no obligation to marry her. To have said no to this foul, wicked soul would have been your salvation. But when she came to you, flaunting her lovely flesh and her extravagant riches, you gave no thought to anything but these illusions and pleasures, and so you sank into the mire of sin and married this woman, who in truth was your own mother.

At this point, Zalman could sit quietly no longer. While he could easily believe all the accusations lodged against Raizel, he considered himself to be innocent—he had been duped by her treacherous wiles.

So Zalman now interrupted Rabbi Israel ben Eliezer, the holy Baal Shem Tov: But holy *tzaddik*, how can you accuse *me*? I was ignorant of these matters when I married my wife. I had no reason to suspect her true nature, and I had no memory of any previous incarnation. I am blameless.

In response, the Baal Shem Tov's face narrowed with rage and his words went forth from his lips like thunder rolling from a storm cloud: How dare you claim to be innocent! When Raizel sought your hand in marriage, did you stop to wonder why—why would a woman so beautiful, so wealthy, who had been married to such a brilliant scholar, stoop to wed you, an ignoramus and a pauper? No, you did not think to ask why, because your sweaty, twitching palms were too eager to run amok upon Raizel's lovely pink flesh. And your belly was bewitched by dreams of moist delicacies, and your neck could not wait to wallow in soft pillows.

Had you reflected wisely, you would have realized that this match must have had some sinister purpose. After all, what had you ever done to merit such extraordinary blessings? Fix a horseshoe? If a miracle wedding could not be due to your merits—and you knew it could not—then it must have been a plot hatched by demons to ensnare you in some wickedness.

But you did not think carefully, no, you jumped eagerly at the pleasures and luxuries Raizel dangled before you, and you married her. On your wedding night, you lay with your own mother, your soul being the son of her soul, and thus committed a dreadful sin. Still, at least there has been no child yet.

Zalman felt as if a wooden beam had been swung into his belly. He fell to the ground in a dizzy haze, and crawled, like a tiny child, to the feet of the Baal Shem Tov. He grabbed the holy man's ankles and pleaded for his soul's repair: But Rabbi, I don't want to sin. I want to follow the Torah. I wish to repent—please, tell me my penance, and I will do it, whatever suffering it may entail.

But the *tzaddik* only spat on Zalman's face and ordered him to be gone. He left Zalman with these words: There is no atonement for you, your soul root is too full of rot, just like your filthy mother.

IX. Confession and Atonement

TRAVELING IN HIS carriage back home, Zalman silently reflected on the Baal Shem Tov's words. He refused to accept that the Gates of Repentance were forever closed to him. How could he have known about souls traveling through many lives and different bodies, about the plots of demon kings and false messiahs, without the holy saint revealing these secrets to him? The Heavenly Court had decreed that he would be born into a poor family, which could not afford to pay for an education that would have provided him with the wisdom necessary to grasp such mysteries.

And why had the saintly Rabbi Israel ben Eliezer, who claimed to know the hidden truth of all these strange events of his life, done nothing before now? If Raizel was so wicked, why hadn't the *tzaddik* somehow sent word to him, warned him not to marry her? But the Baal Shem Tov seemed to prefer watching evil plots unfold in his visions as he reclined in a soft chair in his warm study.

Still, there was one thing that Rabbi Israel had said which gave him hope: His soul had been reincarnated into this body so that he could have the opportunity to lead a pious life in obedience to the commandments of the Torah. And so that was what Zalman decided to do: abandon his wealth and devote his remaining days to prayer, penance, and good deeds.

When he arrived back at his home and saw the surprise on Raizel's face, Zalman realized that, in his intense ruminations, he had forgotten to send word ahead that he was returning from his trip. After recovering her composure, Raizel asked her husband why he appeared to be so troubled—had something gone wrong in his business dealings? Were there unexpected losses?

But instead of responding, Zalman ordered the servants out of the house so he could speak to his wife alone. Raizel sat stiffly in a wooden chair in the kitchen while the muttering servants slowly filed out the door. Looking at her there, he was struck again at how very beautiful she was; even now knowing what she was in the root of her soul, and what terrible crimes she had committed, he could not help feeling drawn to such loveliness.

Once they were alone, Zalman explained that he had not traveled for his business affairs but rather to make a pilgrimage to Rabbi Israel ben Eliezer, the holy Baal Shem Tov. He related everything that he had learned of the roots and histories of their souls, omitting nothing, and concluded by offering her a divorce, as he was going to leave the next day to wander on foot as a beggar and a penitent, suffering and atoning until his soul was cleaved from his body. He urged her also to repent and to devote her remaining days to righteous deeds and charity.

After Zalman had finished, Raizel glared at him intently for a moment, but then she straightened her back and smiled serenely. My dear Zalman, she said, always so full of worry. There is no need to run away. How could you think such a thing? You would trade my beauty, the delicacies of my kitchen, those fine, soft clothes on your back, for . . . for what exactly? Hunger and dirt?

And all because you now think you are damned for being my husband.

Have you considered that perhaps this marriage was Heaven's reward to you? Just because the Baal Shem Tov says you did nothing to merit these blessings, why must you believe him? How do you know that all of his visions come from holy places and not from demons? If the Holy One, Blessed be He, had wanted you to suffer in grinding poverty, He would have made that your fate.

And what about this nonsense that I am your mother? I am barely older than you are—how could I have given birth to you? You had a mother as a little boy, who was not me, and you have told me about her—her borscht, her garlic breath, the faded kerchief soaked with sweat.

And what is this talk of prior incarnations of our souls? Do you remember living a life before this one in a different body? I certainly do not. If we both have no memory of walking this Earth before, who is to say that the man and the woman whom the Baal Shem Tov saw in his vision were truly us? Maybe he has confused us with different souls—after all, there are so many of them floating about, living, dead, waiting to be born.

You need to rest and calm your nerves. Sleep, eat a big, warm breakfast tomorrow. Then all will be well again.

Zalman was moved by her words and wondered why he had been so ready to believe the words that Rabbi Israel ben Eliezer had spoken against her. But then he recalled Raizel's many sins during their marriage: the thefts from the community funds, the mysterious death of the *shammes*, and once more he felt that the Baal Shem Tov's accusations must be true—she was a wicked soul, he knew that without question, so why should he doubt the truth of the holy *tzaddik*'s visions?

So Zalman decided to question Raizel about what the Baal Shem Tov had revealed concerning her conduct in *this* life: Had she poisoned her first husband? Was she the *Pan*'s secret lover? Did he procure the poison for her?

But Raizel just sighed and shook her head: How can you ask such crazy questions? Of course I am not a murderer. Can I say why it is that some live and some die? The Holy One, Blessed be He, decides who will be written in the Book of Life, and He does not ask my advice.

And to think I would take a Polish nobleman as a lover? The *Pan* likes his Gentile women with their thick yellow hair falling down over their shoulders and their immodest dresses flaunting their breasts for his leering eyes. Why would his head be turned by a Jewish matron sweating under her wig? And why would I betray my husband—what joy could I find in arms smeared with bacon grease and vodka?

Zalman asked her again about the poor *shammes*: Hadn't she driven him to his death by some unmentionable, shameful act? Hadn't he seen her that night, with those women in immodest dresses, walking in the moonlight?

But Raizel was unfazed: How should I know, she said, why the *shammes* drowned himself? He did not confide in me. And whatever you thought you saw sounds more like your own dreams drenched in lust. You probably suffered from a nocturnal emission, as I have heard the scholars call it.

Zalman could think of no arguments to hurl back at her—he had seen nothing but stolen glances from a window in the dark— which could have been a dream. Maybe she was right, he could not be sure.

So he ended the conversation, saying he was tired, and went to bed.

In the morning, he ate breakfast with his wife and they made pleasant, idle chatter about everyday matters, cooking, shopping, the weather. Neither of them mentioned their talk from the night before. Zalman felt relieved to pretend, even if just briefly, that nothing had happened.

Later that morning, during his prayers in the synagogue, he reflected again on what to do: Despite the *tzaddik* saying his soul was damned no matter what he did, he still felt he had a choice, either to continue his marriage with Raizel or to forge a new life of penitence. In fact, his thoughts continued, the Baal Shem Tov's insistence that he had no hope of salvation could very well be a test from the Holy One, Blessed be He, to see if Zalman was willing to correct his ways and return to a righteous path even without the promise of a heavenly reward.

If he stayed with Raizel, then upon his death the Heavenly Court would condemn him harshly for choosing to remain with this sinful, wicked woman, as, after everything he had learned, this could only be understood as a deliberate decision to continue to sin.

On the other hand, if he left Raizel, then upon his death the Heavenly Court could condemn him for spurning the great blessings he had been given and for shaming a Jewish bride by divorcing and abandoning her.

So what to do?

Zalman focused again on what he did know for certain: Raizel had twice urged him to steal from community funds, although each time she had given a reason why this little sin would not really harm anyone and would actually, in the long run, help the Jews in the town and surrounding villages.

But no—stealing was wrong. It was a sin. He should have accepted responsibility for his debts, and he should have urged the *Pan* to accept responsibility for his actions too.

He had to leave her. He had to atone for his crimes.

Once his morning prayers had ended, Zalman went to speak with the town rabbi. After they had retired to his study, Zalman asked that the rabbi draw up a *get*, a bill of divorce.

The rabbi protested: Why would Zalman do such a thing? How could his wife have found such disfavor in his eyes—did he really think he could do better than her? And he would be compelled to return her immense dowry, every single ducat. He would be a pauper again. Had he gone mad?

But Zalman replied: I choose freely to be a pauper once more, now and for the rest of my days.

Still, the rabbi pushed back: Why? There must be a reason—men should not just abandon their marriages and run off in rags on some mad whim.

But Zalman would not give a reason. He insisted that his mind was made up, he was leaving that day, and he needed the bill of divorce written out. If the rabbi refused him, then Raizel would become an *agunah*, an abandoned wife unable to remarry because her husband had never delivered a bill of divorce to her.

So the rabbi relented, sighed irritably, and drew up the document. Zalman thanked him and handed over all the coins left in his purse.

Zalman then returned to his home, placed the bill of divorce into a carefully sealed envelope, and left it with the maidservant to deliver later to Raizel.

And Zalman, without a coin left in his pocket, walked away. He picked up a fallen tree branch to use as a walking stick and strolled off along the main road out of the town.

X. Wandering Beggar

ZALMAN AMBLED FOR a long time under the beating sun. After a while, he met a peddler on the road selling clothes, and traded his rich man's clothes for a beggar's rags. By the time he stopped in a new town to pass the night, he had become unrecognizable.

Instead of proceeding to the inn or the synagogue, as he would have formerly done in his wealthy days, Zalman now meekly asked the way to the poorhouse. There he spent the night in a dark corner in a crowded, stuffy room, nibbling on a bit of moldy black bread. The next morning, he continued on his way. And so it went with him: He would not stay the day where he had slept the night. His beard grew wild and dusty, his flesh withered and shrank back to his bones, his feet became a mess of puss-oozing sores, and his skin cracked and reddened under the harsh sun.

And there was always hunger in his belly. His body pled with his soul to return to Raizel and be reconciled—to find a way to return to warm blankets and succulent brisket and sweet wine.

But Zalman's soul rebuked his weak flesh: We must atone, for we have sinned greatly.

With so little food in his stomach, Zalman's mind could no longer focus; faces, roads, towns, all became a blur. When he had first become a beggar, he had asked for alms in a clearly articulated, albeit exaggeratedly submissive, voice. But soon enough, his voice thinned out, his dusty lungs grew weak, and he could barely manage more than a whisper. In his meekness, he looked to other people, the loud and the well fed, to tell him where to go and what to do.

Yet there was one thing that he did make a point of asking in each new town, even though he had to struggle to heave the words up his throat and past his lips: Were there any sick or dead for whom he could recite Psalms?

If the answer from the *shammes* of the town's synagogue was yes—and it often was—Zalman would borrow a prayer book and spend the night, usually alone, on a synagogue bench reciting Psalms until his strength gave way and he collapsed from exhaustion.

Sometimes during these dark, solitary nights he would hear moaning sounds in the synagogue, and he would see hulking shadows sliding along the moonlit walls, almost as if they were Jews swaying with their prayers. These were the dead, Zalman thought, come to join me in reciting Psalms for their grandchildren.

In the morning, the families for whose relative he had prayed would offer to pay Zalman in gratitude for the Psalms he had recited all through the night. But he always refused. Being able to perform the *mitzvah*, the good deed, he would say in his rasping voice, was payment enough.

In reply, the finely dressed Jewish householders would put their hands on his shoulders and bathe him in warm, approving smiles. He felt, at these moments, that he had finally become a good man, a pious man.

Sometimes he was asked his name. After all, these householders would say, even if he refused their money, they at least wanted to thank him properly.

But Zalman would never reveal his true name, lest he be recognized as a formerly wealthy merchant. He worried that, if they knew the truth, the rich men whom he met would try to lift him back up in the world to where they would feel he naturally belonged. So he would squeak out in his whispering voice one of many aliases he thought up: Itzik, Yankel, Yoschke, Mayerl, and so on. He enjoyed being unknown: It seemed to make the erasure of his past sins more complete.

Having destroyed every last vestige of the sinner he had once been, Zalman now waited peacefully for his death. At some point soon, he was sure, his emaciated body would become sick. Perhaps when winter comes, he thought; yes, when winter comes and his bare, blistered feet sink deep into the snowdrifts, then his flesh will yield up to a final sickness.

He saw it vividly in his mind: He would be walking on a road, when a hard, icy rain would suddenly pour down upon him. His soaked body would shiver and tremble, his teeth would chatter miserably, and then the coughing would start—a little at first, but soon worse, much worse, until he would find himself spitting up spoonfuls of blood. There would be sharp pains in his chest, a raging fever, and rivers of sweat.

And then at last, there would be a rustling sound nearby, and his eyes would open one last time. Standing over him would be an immense figure in a black hooded robe with a hundred eyes peeking out in grim determination. The Angel of Death would raise his long knife and swiftly cut Zalman's windpipe, in a proper kosher slaughter.

His soul would then ascend to the World to Come to be judged before the Heavenly Court. The accusing angel, a foul creature with a birdlike face and beady eyes, twitching with disgust at humanity and all its crimes, would passionately denounce Zalman for his sins, describing each one in perfect detail, omitting nothing. And Zalman's soul would tremble with fear.

But then the defending angel would rise up, tall, broad-shouldered, with a tremendous grey beard. He would grant the accusing angel his due: This soul had indeed blackened itself with sin. Nonetheless, he would continue, the accused had abandoned his sinful ways, and afflicted and mortified himself in atonement. He had lived a life of simple piety, giving his prayers generously to those in need but taking nothing in return.

The attendants at the Heavenly Tribunal would then bring out the golden scales. First the accusing angel would empty his bag of sins upon one side of the scales, and they would tip heavily towards conviction. The accusing angel would smile his malicious smile, smugly certain of his triumph.

But then the defending angel would empty his bag of *mitzvot*, good deeds, onto the other side. The scales would swing wildly, up and down, the outcome uncertain, until, at the very last moment, the defending angel would luckily remember one more good deed—a night of Psalm reading for the soul of a sick girl, such heartfelt prayers that they had moved the Throne of Glory to cancel the cruel decree to take the girl's life—and that one additional good deed would tip the scales decisively in favor of Zalman's redemption.

Judgment would then be entered upon the verdict: Zalman's soul could enter Paradise.

Such were the honeyed dreams of the wandering beggar as he forced his blistered, bleeding feet across a hot, dusty road.

XI. Judgment

ZALMAN ARRIVED IN the *shtetl* of T. on a late Friday afternoon and made his way to the large synagogue near the town square. Once there, he shuffled quietly to the back benches to recite Psalms. He assumed that the *shammes* of the synagogue would approach him at some point to steer him towards the poorhouse for the night.

However, when this *shammes* eventually came around, his manner was not brusque or impatient, as Zalman would have expected, but instead yielding and almost submissive. The *shammes* explained that there was a wealthy woman in this town who, to atone for her past sins and to merit her portion in the World to Come, insisted that every wandering beggar eat at her table. And not merely eat, the *shammes* continued, but eat like a king, like an emperor: heaps of delicacies and endless cups of fine wine, with servants washing your hands and feet, seated in a place of honor at the head of the table. When you have eaten and drunk your fill, the good lady gives you a thick warm blanket to sleep under in her barn.

But Zalman demurred: I have no desire for rich food and drink. I need only a crust of bread and a sip of water to keep body and soul stitched together.

The *shammes* urged him to reconsider—surely it is permitted to have a little taste of happiness in this life; after all, delicacies and fine wines were also created by *HaShem* in His Infinite Goodness, just like bread, water, and Psalms. Picture it in your mind, succulent roasted goose, brisket, kugel, washed down by sweet Hungarian wine, eh, just imagine that . . .

And Zalman did imagine it: the words of the *shammes* brought to mind the foods he had eaten when he had been a rich man, and he could almost smell them again, and feel their warm, soft textures on his tongue. His belly now moaned and begged louder than ever for a night of such pleasures, just one evening in which it could be happily stuffed again.

Just one evening, Zalman mused. Would the Heavenly Tribunal count it against me if I had one last decent meal before I die? And I would be helping this woman atone by letting her give charity. Am I so arrogant as to scorn a kind hand offering me a slight reprieve from my sufferings?

So Zalman agreed to dine at the wealthy woman's table. Beaming from ear to ear, the *shammes* led him from the synagogue to a large house on the town's outskirts. Once they were inside the vestibule, the *shammes* loudly announced that Zalman was a wandering beggar who had traveled to their town for the *Shabbat* holiday, and then he slipped away.

A stout maidservant, smelling strongly of soap, now took charge of Zalman. With grim determination, she washed his feet and hands, gave him a pair of shoes to wear (although they were too big for his feet), and sat him down in a lushly upholstered chair at the head of a long table.

To his amazement, Zalman was asked to recite the *kiddush* before the meal. He stumbled through the prayer as best he could—he had not had to recite it himself in a long time—but none of the servants hovering about mocked him or grew impatient. To the contrary, he was honored as if he were the most eminent scholar visiting from the most famous *yeshiva*.

The meal was everything that the *shammes* had promised: a plate piled so high with warm, crunchy *schnitzel* that the pieces were falling off the sides of the dish; a thick and tasty potato soup; more slices of honey cake than he could count; and cup after cup of sweet plum brandy to wash it all down.

Yet there was something peculiar about this *Shabbat* dinner: No one joined him to share in all this abundance. At first, Zalman had wanted to ask where the lady of the house was, if only to thank her for her gracious hospitality, but he was soon too busy devouring his food and drink to think about anything else.

As the evening wore on, the strong brandy made Zalman light-headed and dizzy. His limbs grew heavy, and he could no longer feel his fingers or his toes. Increasingly exhausted by his intense gluttony, he struggled to keep his head up and his eyes open. When the weariness in his bones finally became too great, his head crashed down on the table, splattering a piece of cake, and then darkness enveloped him.

At one point, Zalman had the vague sensation of being lifted and carried, but he was not sure if that had been real or a dream.

When he awoke again, Zalman found himself lying naked on top of a luxurious bed. There were thick curtains encircling the mattress and bedposts, so that he was unable to tell if it was day or night. He tried to sit up, but then felt something tight pinning his arms in place.

With just enough of a sliver of a light coming through the curtains, he saw that his arms had been tied with rope to the bed. When he tried to move his legs, he quickly realized that they too had been bound.

Terror seized Zalman's heart. Perhaps, he thought, demons had kidnapped him and dragged him to some desolate swamp and everything around him was an illusion. He had been tempted back into sin, stuffing himself greedily with the demons' foods, luxuriating in fleshly delights, and now he was to suffer his punishment.

He cried out for help as loudly as he could, but he doubted if anyone would be able to hear him. After a while his screams petered out and he lay still and silent behind the dark curtains. He thought that this must have been how the Prophet Jonah felt when he was floating in the belly of the whale.

But then there was the sound of a door creaking open and feet slowly walking across the floor. Zalman's body tensed; a thousand horrors raced through his mind and his heart thumped wildly. He wanted to shout out to whoever was there, but fear strangled the words in his throat.

The feet stopped moving. He heard light breathing, and then a sigh—a woman's sigh.

The curtains moved, and pale, delicate hands—the sort of hands that performed no labor—appeared to his eyes. As the curtains spread apart, he saw a woman with a thick veil. She sat down on the edge of the bed and stroked his cheek.

Zalman looked up at her and was flooded with tenderness. He wondered if he had died and if this was a kind angel who had come to take him to Paradise. Perhaps his penance had been accepted by the Throne of Glory and his trials of atonement were complete.

But then she removed her veil and Zalman beheld his former wife Raizel. The shock made him flinch and fear again seized hold of his heart.

My dearest Zalman, she said calmly, I always knew you would return to me. You are my *bashert*, destined from birth to be my bridegroom. I had rejected so many other matches because I knew I was fated to find happiness only with you, that my children could only have one true father, and that he was you.

I gave you everything: wealth, honor, the delights of my flesh. And even though you, a poor blacksmith, had nothing to give to me in return, that was fine. As King Solomon sang to his bride: I am my beloved's and my beloved is mine.

And yet you fled from my arms.

Well, to be precise, you fled twice. You first fled to Rabbi Israel ben Eliezer, the Baal Shem Tov, who told you wicked, horrible lies about me. And you *chose* to believe these slanders—you, my *bashert*, my destined one, you chose to believe what you were told by a stranger instead of defending me, your beloved.

By this point, Zalman had recovered himself enough to try to mount a defense: How could I not believe him? The Baal Shem Tov, may his merit protect us, is a holy *tzaddik*, a saint, deeply learned in mystical knowledge and hidden matters. You and your father believed in the truth of his visions—that is why you visited him. You believed him when he told you that I was your destined bridegroom.

A harshness now crept over Raizel's features, and her fingers bent towards her palms like claws on a bird of prey. He could hear her hard, fast breaths. When she spoke, there was anger in her voice:

I believed him, because when he spoke your name to me, my heart trembled. Hearing that you were my destined bridegroom was like listening to a man say the sky is blue or the river is wet. This truth was so obvious that I could not conceive how anyone could doubt it.

When he slandered me, did you have the same feeling? The Baal Shem Tov spun a mad tale to you about your soul's previous incarnation when you supposedly were my son. Did you remember those events from a prior incarnation? If your soul had truly lived through them, how could it have forgotten? I certainly recall nothing from any earlier incarnation of my soul.

And what of his silly tale that I had seduced the *Pan*, Count Jan P.? Did you ever see me travel to His Lordship's manor house? If he was my lover, don't you think I would have called upon him after he returned to his estates, to renew our debauchery? But no, the only one summoned by the *Pan* was you.

Zalman now interjected again, his voice wavering a bit: But Raizel, what does any of this matter? I sinned—I stole from community funds. I needed to repent. And I did not abandon you. I gave you a *get*, a bill of divorce, so you could remarry, find yourself a better groom. You are young, beautiful, wealthy—you said yourself that there were many fine Jews who had wanted your hand but that it was *you* who had rejected them. You could go back to your pile of discarded matches and pick out the one that pleases you best.

Raizel's body shook violently, and Zalman could hear the rage in her voice when she answered him:

You did not have to leave me in order to repent. I told you how to atone for what were, at most, trivial indiscretions: just replace the money you had withdrawn from the community coffers as soon as you could. You did that once. If your sin was theft, then your penance was restitution.

You left me because you no longer saw your beautiful bride. You saw only the lies which dribbled out of the mouth of Rabbi Israel ben Eliezer, the Baal Shem Tov, may that wretched slanderer be cursed and damned. And that is why you fled—because you chose to believe those lies about your beloved and you chose to despise her.

And you think I should be grateful for the bill of divorce? You seem quite proud of yourself for divorcing me—as if the divorce was a *mitzvah*, a righteous deed, proof of your kindness and compassion even to the depraved monster who had shared your wedding bed.

How could I marry again? One husband dead, and another divorced me and fled in secret, as if I was a vicious snake about to murder him with my venom. Do you think the matchmakers pounded down my door again? No one spoke to me again of fine, distinguished matches.

To be more precise, no one spoke to me at all. But even when you are spoken of only in hushed whispers behind your back, those whispers have a way of floating about in the air until they rest on your shoulder and unburden themselves into your ears. And what did those whispers say to me? That I had murdered my first husband and my second husband had fled for his life. After all, what else could make a man like you, a nothing, a pauper, abandon a beautiful and wealthy bride? It could only be that I was so terrible, so hideous, that my loveliness and riches were not sufficient compensation for the sufferings I had inflicted upon my unfortunate husbands.

I locked myself in my bedroom and I wept until I had no more tears left. I begged the Angel of Death to put an end to my agony.

But I was cursed to live on.

I asked myself, why am I decreed to continue to live? If I am so awful, why not cut me down like a poisonous weed in the field and toss me into the burning tar pits of *gehenna*? And then the truth of the matter was revealed to me, with the clarity of a vision that could only have come from the Holy One, Blessed be He: I must live in order to force your atonement—I must become the instrument of your real penance.

For you had sinned against me, gravely. I would have no husband now and I would never bear children. You had been destined to be my happiness and yet you discarded me. You killed our children before they ever had a chance to smile and kiss their mama's cheeks.

Yes, you had sinned greatly against me. And now I knew that I must make you atone.

So I picked myself up from my bed, washed away the tracks of my dried tears, sold all my belongings, and moved far away to a town where no one would know me. I changed my name and hid my face behind a thick veil.

I knew you had left without any money, so I assumed you would turn to begging and wandering. Thus I told the *shammes* at the synagogue here that I would give him a gold ducat for each new wandering beggar whom he persuaded to receive charity at my table.

But even if I could get you here, how would I ensure that you would properly, and fully, atone for your many sins against me? Well, you had already suggested the answer to me: You told me that Rabbi Israel ben Eliezer, the Baal Shem Tov, had said that I had seduced the *Pan* in order to procure poison to murder my first husband. I decided that forcing you to live your own lies would be your fitting penance.

So I bribed one of the servants of the nobleman who rules these lands to obtain an audience with His Lordship. Once we were alone, I removed my veil and my shawl, letting the filthy *goy* drink in my loveliness. He could not control himself and we became lovers that afternoon.

But when he later sent word that he wished for my favors again, I replied there was a price: I needed a small, but highly effective, phial of poison, to pour down the throat of my wicked husband, who had treated me cruelly.

My new lover was only too happy to oblige.

Raizel now reached into the drawer of a small table next to the bed and removed a tiny, greenish bottle. She pulled out the stopper and leaned over him as if to pour its contents into his mouth. Zalman shut his lips tightly and turned away in terror.

But she calmly reached over with her right hand and squeezed his nose with a strength that he never knew she possessed. Zalman was forced to open his mouth to breathe.

No sooner had his lips parted then Raizel shoved the bottle between them and poured the green liquid down his throat. Soon he felt a great weight crushing his chest, and his lungs and heart were paralyzed.

For a moment, the world went dark.

And then he could see again. Raizel had gone and gone too were the thick curtains. But at the foot of the bed Zalman saw a black hooded figure with a hundred eyes and a long knife. The Angel of Death had come for him.

Other Books by Barak Bassman

Elegy of the Minotaur

Repentance: A Tale of Demons in Old Jewish Poland

King Solomon and Ashmedai: A Wisdom Tale

The Twilight of the Magical Siren: A Tale of Late Antiquity

The Leper Princess and The Court Jew

The Last Confession of Joseph della Reina

The Gifts of the Fairy Melusine

*Necromancy of the Demon Maiden:
A Gothic Tale of Podolia*

The Death of the Wizard Merlin

The Vampire and The Wandering Jew

The Emissary from Mezeritch: A Dark Hasidic Tale

The Beheading Game: An Arthurian Tale

9 781956 867060